THE HEART
OF DARKNESS
CLUB
A NOVEL

GARY REILLY

Running Meter Press
DENVER

This is the third book in the The Asphalt Warrior series.
The fourth book in the series, *Home for the Holidays*, is scheduled for release in November 2013

This is a work of fiction. Any resemblance of characters to actual persons, living or dead, is purely coincidental.

Published by
Running Meter Press
2509 Xanthia St.
Denver, CO 80238
Publisher@RunningMeterPress.com
720 328 5488

Cover art by John Sherffius
Composition by D. Kari Luraas

ISBN: 978-0-9847860-2-2

Library of Congress Control Number: 2013930623

First Edition 2013

Printed in the United States of America

Other Titles in The Asphalt Warrior Series

The Asphalt Warrior
Ticket to Hollywood

CHAPTER 1

I pulled into the cabstand at the Fairmont Hotel just as a call came over the radio. There were five cabs ahead of me at the stand so I figured I had better take the call. If there had been four cabs I would have settled in with my Coke and Twinkie and paperback book, but five cabs meant that the waiting time for a fare to come out of the hotel would have been too long in terms of the "Work/Loaf Ratio" that I have spent fourteen years perfecting as a taxi driver on the mean streets of Denver. I won't bore you with a long-winded explanation of the "W/LR" save to say that it is an algebraic formula of such complex numeric subtlety that it can be understood only by mathematicians and hobos.

"One twenty-seven," I said into the microphone.

"Eight-fourteen Tremont," the dispatcher said. "Party named Trowbridge. He'll be waiting outside."

"Check."

I hung up the mike and pulled out of the cabstand and drove down the street. A couple of the taxis were Rocky Cab hacks. I knew what the drivers were thinking: Murph knows something. Whenever a cabbie jumps a bell from a cabstand, the other cabbies think he knows something. Vail trip, they think. A rich businessman going to Denver International Airport, they think. They think anybody fool enough to abandon the security of a cabstand must be hip to a jackpot. I like people to mistakenly assume good things about me. It enhances my rep.

It took one minute to get to the Tremont address. I saw the guy waiting outside the building, but he was no businessman. It's easy to recognize businessmen. They wear suits and vote Republican. It's true that this guy was wearing what could loosely be defined as a "suit," if you think of Bozo the Clown as wearing a suit. Unmatched sports jacket, baggy pants, and dusty shoes, plus unkempt hair. That's all you need to know. He was standing in the midst of what I took to be all of his worldly possessions. My heart sank.

Every so often I get one of those people. "Movers" as they are referred to by us cabbies, although they are not to be confused with "movers and shakers." Movers are people who think a taxicab is Mayflower Van Lines. They are people forced by tragic circumstances to flee their current residence and find someplace else to live. Their modus operandi is always the same. They give a little wave signaling that they called the cab, then they begin loading your trunk with their stuff. They disappear into their apartment building and come out with more stuff. There's usually a shabby suitcase or two. My heart sinks when I realize I've got a mover on my hands because he or she usually has an apartment lined up not far away, so the fare comes to only three or four dollars. It's worse than a supermarket run, because shoppers rarely have as much stuff as movers.

But my heart goes out to these people even as it's sinking, which is scientifically feasible as I know from experience. Out and down, that's where my heart went when I pulled up to the curb. I couldn't tell if the guy was older than me. It's always a shock to find myself in the presence of desperate people my own age. When I was a kid I always assumed that bums, losers, and grandparents had to be at least fifty years old.

"I have a few more things inside," the guy said as he thrust his shabby suitcase into my trunk along with a cardboard box filled with the twisted remains of his life. I nodded. I knew the drill. There's nothing you can say. You know you're in for at least a half-hour of downtime, meaning you won't be jumping any good bells for the next thirty minutes. It's sort of like waiting for a bus to nowhere except you're the driver.

I watched the guy disappear into the building. It was an old nineteenth-century Denver building, a five-story, red brick joint that had an appointment with the wrecking ball. The upper stories were apartments, and the ground-floor space had been a lot of things in its time, including an X-rated magazine store. I knew this because when I was a student at nearby UCD, I sometimes walked past this building on the way to a bar after class, but I never had the guts to step inside. (The word around the English department hinted that the store traded in 1950s *Playboys*, but nobody knew for sure.)

When Trowbridge came back outside with his arms loaded down with more stuff I worked a pleasant smile onto my face, but he didn't look at me. He was embarrassed, I could tell—me and embarrassment are old pals. I didn't offer to help him carry any of his stuff. That's the unwritten code between cabbies and movers. It may sound cruel, but that's the way the game is played. The cabby pretends to be miffed, and the mover is required to feel embarrassed. It's his punishment for tricking the cab driver into playing Mayflower, because he knows he's not going to give you a tip, and so do you.

When I say the cabbie pretends to be miffed, the truth is that the cabbie really is miffed, but only at himself for getting roped into a lousy trip. Cabbies are like gamblers. They hate to lose, but you'll notice that they never walk away from the craps table. And do you know why? It's because they believe that after they drop off the short fare they will get a Vail trip to balance their bad luck. Does the phrase "God is on my side" ring a bell? The worst part of being a cabbie gambler is that, unlike a Vegas gambler or a dog-track gambler, cabbies always break even. By this I mean you can tear your hair out over a short fare or click your heels over a trip to Vail, but at the end of the fiscal year you still average seventy lousy bucks per day. Fifty, if you happen to be me. You can't win in this game, but you can't lose either. It's sort of like high school—you can loaf through four years or study your ass off, but in the end everybody is handed the same ol' sheepskin.

"Where to?" I said.

"Five-sixteen Curtis," he replied.

A two-buck trip tops—it was almost a record.

I once got a call at a motel on east Colfax where a woman was moving from her motel room to a room in a motel next door. It was my first
experience with a mover and I was staggered. I was thirty-one years old.
I was fairly new at cab driving. The woman was around the same age as
me, I could tell. After I got over my shock and outrage, my heart went
out to her. She really seemed embarrassed. I helped her carry some boxes.
I didn't know the rules. The fare came to a dollar-sixty. After I dropped
her off, I drove away wondering what she would be doing when she was
forty-five. You already know what I'm doing.

I pulled up at the Curtis address. It was another old, red brick building. The meter came to two dollars and twenty cents. Trowbridge leaned
over the back of my seat and held out a crisp new five-dollar bill. I took
it and reached into my shirt pocket for change but he said, "Keep it,"
and waved a horizontal palm as if shooing away pigeons. This made
me feel bad. The guy obviously had taken similar trips and knew how
cranky some cabbies could get about short trips. Me, I keep my cranki-
ness to myself. Short trips come with the territory—and there actually
is something to the belief that the next trip might end up a Vail trip. By
"Vail trip" I mean any long trip that will bring the average of this hour's
take to fifteen bucks. Everything evens out in the world of cab driving,
unfortunately.

I did hop out though and help remove some boxes from the trunk,
just to acknowledge the 115 percent tip. But I only set them on the sidewalk. I knew this was what he would want without asking. I could sense
that, in his own way, he was an old pro and did not need or want help
carrying his stuff into his newest awful digs. He got right to work hauling
the boxes into the foyer and setting them down and striding back out to
retrieve the rest of his stuff. He knew his business.

"Need any help?" I said, just to bring closure to the tip.

"No thank you, I'm fine," he said. It had a practiced sound. I nodded and climbed back into 127 and drove away. As I pulled up at a red light, I took a deep breath and said with a sigh, "There but for the grace of God, etc." I sigh that quite frequently. I have no idea what my life would be like or what I would be doing for a living if it wasn't for cab driving, but I suspect it would involve manual labor. Who the hell invented cab driving anyway? A Pharaoh?

As I wended my way back toward the Fairmont I began to wonder what age Trowbridge was. He could have been younger than me but not by much. Sitting in a cab all day doing nothing has helped me to age well, unlike, for instance, a farmer battling hail and cows. Trowbridge had looked old, but that was partly due to his clothes and wild hair and four o'clock shadow. I myself sport a ponytail. The chicks tell me it makes me look younger. My male friends say it makes me look like I'm not "with it," meaning ponytails are "out" and have been, I guess, since the sixties. But after disco was invented, I pretty much lost interest in American cultural innovation. For some reason, I still feel the same age I was when I began driving a cab fourteen years ago. As I overtly implied, I'm forty-five years old. I'll never forget the day I turned thirty-seven. On that day I said to myself, "I'm the same age as James Bond." It was one of the biggest thrills of my life, so you can imagine how thrilling my life is.

CHAPTER 2

I was fifty bucks to the good when I called it quits that evening. Just to clarify things for people who have no grasp of cab driving, it costs me seventy bucks a day to lease my cab at the motor, which is what we call the cab company. I also pour ten dollars' worth of gas into the tank at dawn, so I have to earn at least eighty bucks before I start seeing any profit. It's always a kick when I hit the eighty-one-dollar mark, but I usually blow the first buck on a lottery scratch ticket. Call me a cockeyed optimist, but I've had my fingers crossed ever since the Colorado legislature legalized stupidity.

I have a friend named Big Al who holds nothing but contempt for the lottery, which strikes me as strange because he's a gambler—plays the dogs, the horses, poker, etc. I've never played poker with him and never will. He wins. He also wins at the track. Not always, but always enough. I would think that, to him, the lottery would be like the slots in Vegas, where he goes twice a year to "clear out the sewage" as he puts it. He has told me that slots are what he plays to relax from the craps and blackjack tables. I have never played craps and do not want to learn, although I once lost three hundred dollars playing blackjack. There is no story there. I just lost.

I do watch craps games during my occasional trips through Reno to California, where I go every so often to visit my evil brother Gavin, who is a businessman with a real job. Craps requires a rudimentary comprehension of mathematics, which automatically disqualifies me from playing. Eighty-one dollars and a lottery ticket I can understand. Fifty bucks profit I can understand. But when it comes to the esoteric nature of odds, I'm like one of those skiers you read about in the papers who was last seen trying to outrace an avalanche—the body is dug up come spring. Remind me to tell you the story about the day I walked away from a slot machine jackpot because I was late for a transcontinental bus.

I drove back to the Rocky Mountain Taxicab Company (RMTC) a little before seven P.M. I had pulled a twelve-hour shift, had my fifty-dollar minimum quota of profit, and was ready to head home and relax in front of my TV. Things had been going like this for the past couple of months. Profitable days and quiet nights. Somehow I had avoided getting involved in the personal lives of my fares during that time, although it was no accident. I had made a conscious effort, which is rare for me. Without going into too much detail, my life sometimes gets complicated when I make the mistake of trying to help people who have problems that are too overwhelming for them to deal with by themselves. Given my age, sex, educational background, and income bracket, I do not know what makes me think I am qualified to help anybody do anything. Big Al tells me it's because I have no control over my rampant ego, but I like to think it's because I'm bored. However, sometimes people actually do ask me for advice.

I was shocked the first time a fare asked me for advice. I had been driving a taxi for only two weeks. Back then I didn't know that I would be driving a taxi for the next fourteen years. I thought it was just a temporary gig until I sold my first novel, but let's not get into that.

The guy who asked me for advice was younger than me, and said his family wanted him to become a doctor, except he didn't really want to go to medical school. He asked me what to do. I thought he was nuts—I was just a cab driver, not a career counselor. To jump ahead here a little bit, I eventually came to realize that most people seem to think that all cab drivers are founts of wisdom. But I also learned that the amount of advice a cab driver hands out can affect the size of his tip. Maybe I do understand mathematics. At any rate, being a beginner with no practical knowledge of anything at all, I told the kid that he should do only what he wanted to do—and I added that, personally, I wouldn't want my appendix removed by somebody who wasn't in the mood. He tipped me four bucks. My education as a cab driver had begun in earnest.

I learned my lessons well, but the most valuable lesson I learned was to avoid getting involved in the personal lives of my fares. Some people call it "the road to hell." It's funny how true clichés can be. I don't know why English professors criticize clichés. I've never met a cliché I didn't like, which may explain why I've been an unpublished novelist for twenty years.

But I was feeling pretty good when I dropped off my taxi for the night. I entered the on-call room at Rocky Cab and turned in my tripsheet and key. The day-man in the cage, Rollo, had already gone home, which made me feel good. Me and Rollo don't see eye-to-eye on everything. The night-man had already come on duty. His name was Stew. It still is. He's a model-railroading buff. 'Nuff said on that subject.

As I say, I was feeling pretty good when I got off duty. I climbed into my heap, a black 1964 Chevy with red doors, and drove back to my apartment on Capitol Hill. I live on the top floor of a three-story apartment building, which was some sort of millionaire's mansion back in the nineteenth century. I don't know who lived on the top floor back in those days, but I like to think it was the scullery maid. It's a cozy dump. I call it my "crow's nest." I can see the rooftops of the city from up there. I parked in the dirt lot behind the house and climbed the rear fire escape and entered by the back door, which opens directly into the kitchen. I set my cab accouterment on the table and entered the living room and walked over to one of my many bookshelves where I pulled out my copy of Finnegans Wake. That's where I stash my cab profits. I plucked my take out of my shirt pocket and started to stuff it into the book, but then I noticed some handwriting on the back of one of the bills.

I recognized the bill. It was the crisp new fiver handed to me by the mover, Mister Trowbridge. I don't get that many crisp fivers on the job. Don't ask me why, except that people who take cabs rarely give me "crispies," as we hacks call new bills. There are basically two classes of people who take cabs: poor people and rich people. The middle class tends to stay out of the whole mess. Poor people for the most part can't afford their own cars, and the rich simply don't drive themselves to the airport, which is practically the only place I've ever taken a rich person. There are exceptions of course, but the middle class have a tendency to drive themselves wherever they go. I've never fully understood why anybody goes anywhere, but I suppose if I was middle class, I would probably go somewhere, too.

I held up the fiver to get a better look at it. I could see the details pretty well. I wear bifocal contact lenses. The printing was small, cramped, and squared, and looked relatively fresh, so I got the feeling that Trowbridge had written the words, especially when I read what the English professors refer to as the "content," which went as follows: "You must wake up each day in a state of total despair."

I stood in the silence of my crow's nest pondering these words. Due to the fact that I am a graduate of the University of Colorado at Denver with a Bachelor's degree in English, I began to parse the sentence. This is what English majors do. It's what we're trained to do. We don't know how to do anything else, except drive cabs. But I couldn't quite nail down the exact nature of the statement. Maybe Trowbridge had simply written a note to himself, like one of those reminders that you see on preprinted tablets that say "Things To Do Today."

Why would a guy like Trowbridge have to remind himself to do a thing like that? One look in a mirror ought to be enough.

I pondered the word "must." It had the connotation of a command rather than a polite suggestion, i.e., "You must wake up in a state of total despair, or all is lost."

I shrugged and started to put the bill into my *Finnegans,* but then my esoteric knowledge of sentence structure, combined with my inherent paranoia, suddenly gave me pause. It occurred to me that Trowbridge might have been making an observation about me—"By the look of my cab driver, I can only conclude that he must wake up each day in a state of total despair."

I could picture Trowbridge sitting in the backseat staring at my ponytail, and then … passing judgment!

It gave me the willies.

I jammed the fiver into the book and closed it. I set the book on the shelf and went back into the kitchen and started to fry up a burger for supper. *Gilligan's Island* was scheduled to start in a few minutes and I didn't want to miss the opening song. I'll admit it. I always sing along with the theme song. Who doesn't? Women maybe.

When *Gilligan's Island* first appeared on TV, I was a kid living in Wichita, Kansas, where I was born. I thought Bob Denver was the lead singer of The Wellingtons, the group that recorded the song. I guess this was what my Maw was talking about when she talked about the superiority of radio over television, and how radio forces the listener to use his imagination. There seemed to be something Bob Denverish about the lead singer's voice. I later discovered to my dismay that he was not a part of the group. But since Bob Denver had once played the role of Maynard G. Krebbs on *The Many Loves of Dobie Gillis,* I imagined him looking like a beatnik and playing an acoustic guitar and singing the song while Sherwood Schwartz sat at the controls in the recording booth. That tells you everything you need to know about my imagination, and my Maw.

I flipped the burger once and accidentally flattened it on the frying pan with the spatula, but I kept thinking about that fiver in my *Finnegans.* I finally set the spatula down and went back into the living room and pulled the book off the shelf. I opened it and took the bill out and reread the sentence. Then I set the book back on the shelf and reached for my copy of *The Stranger* by Albert Camus. I placed the fiver inside, and put it back on the shelf.

I decided I wanted to hold onto the bill for awhile. I didn't want to spend it until I came to grips with both the message and the audience. Had Trowbridge written it to himself, or to me? The possibility of ever learning the truth was nil, which was why I felt it belonged in my Camus. One thing I had learned in college was that if you ever had a question about truth, reality, or the meaning of existence, read a novel by Albert Camus. Pretty soon you'll be so baffled you'll forget the question.

(For those of you who never served in the army and subsequently faked your way through seven years of college, "Camus" rhymes with "Shamu" [the killer whale]).

But merely opening *The Stranger* had helped me. Five minutes later I was seated in front of my TV with a beer and a burger, waiting for the tantalizing vision of Mary Ann to come sashaying down the beach in her tight denim short-shorts. I don't know who invented the word "sashay," but Mary Ann brought it to life and gave it meaning. She always makes me forget Albert Camus.

CHAPTER 3

Three days later I had a rare run of good luck. I picked up a businessman at the Hilton Hotel and he uttered the magic acronym: "DIA." I pocketed fifty-five dollars at the drop-off point at the airport terminal, then I took a quick run down to the staging area to buy a Coke from a machine.

The staging area is far away from the terminal, out in a kind of weed field. It's a little island of asphalt where the cabbies wait anywhere from three to five hours for a fifty-dollar trip back to Denver. I did that a few times after DIA opened for business, hoping that somehow I could squeeze in three trips per day. One hundred and fifty bucks for a day's work would have suited me fine, but it was like trying to beat the house odds in Reno. All I needed at the airport was just one extra tiny little hour to make my scheme work, but the gods laughed at me. Two trips per day was all I could eke out, so I gave it up and went back to what is loosely defined in the taxi business as "work." Hotels and bells, that's what the gods had in mind for this ponytailed Odysseus.

Okay. Here's my Reno story:

I was headed to San Francisco on a bus, and we made a short stop in a little town near Wendover. To kill half an hour, I climbed off the bus and wandered into a casino, which was virtually deserted. It was almost noon, and I had my pick of the slots. I decided to try my luck at a quarter machine near a window where I could keep my eye on the bus parked across the street. I was new at the game and wasn't familiar with the payoffs, which were printed on a metal plaque on the front of the machine for reasons that I never understood. Who reads machines?

The slot I chose to play had a metal pole sticking out of its top and was cluttered with colored lights like an artificial Christmas tree. I didn't know what it was there for. I didn't know anything about slots, but I knew how to put money into a hole. I had been doing that all my life.

So I stood there and poured quarters in and pulled the handle and won and lost small amounts. Pretty soon passengers started climbing onto the bus, so I figured it was time to go. I shoved my last quarter into the slot and pulled the lever, and as I did this I saw the driver come out the door of a little café and climb onto the bus, so I figured I had better get out of the casino. And then it happened.

The wheels on the slot machine stopped spinning and suddenly the Christmas tree lit up. The pole began rotating. I didn't know what the hell was going on. But the bus was about to leave and I didn't have time to read the goddamned knowledge plaque. I waited a few seconds to see if any quarters came pouring out of the machine but nothing happened. So as they say in the far West, I "hightailed it" out of the casino and ran across the street and hopped onto the bus just before the driver closed the door.

I made my way to the backseat of the bus where I always sleep on cross-country trips, and looked out the rear window. I could see the Christmas tree revolving through the tinted window of the casino. The bus pulled onto the road and headed out of town. I knelt on the backseat and watched the flashing colored lights grow smaller and smaller as we made our way into the empty wastelands of the desert.

A week later I was back in Denver and I ran into Big Al, who was parked in the cab line outside the Brown Palace Hotel. I told him about the casino and the flashing lights and the rotating pole and the mad dash to the bus. After I finished relating my vivid narrative, he stared at me in silence.

I began to grow nervous.

"Do ... you ... have ... any ... idea ... what ... you ... did?" he said slowly and distinctly.

"No," I said. "I don't know anything about slot machines. That was the first time I ever played one."

Big Al refused to speak to me for a month. He never did explain to me exactly what I did, but I sort of figured it out by myself.

After I got to the DIA staging area, I parked 127 in a slot adjacent to the cinderblock building where they have pop and candy machines and restrooms, plus it's the place where the DIA personnel send cabbies up to the terminal. The DIA dispatcher sits at a window like a ticket booth at a movie theater, and manipulates a system of traffic lights to signal the drivers when they can go. It's complicated. The building reminds me of the Nevada casino. It's out in the middle of nowhere.

I put fifty cents into a slot and won a Coke, then I stepped outside the building and looked at the scores of taxis waiting for the signal to drive up to the terminal. The cabbies were either seated inside their hacks, or standing around discussing politics and women. It looked like an annual convention of town loafers. I've been there.

I climbed into 127 and drove away. I took Peña Boulevard to I-70, and then a call came over the radio for a fare waiting at a 7-11 store nearby. Normally I don't jump 7-11 bells because half the time the callers disappear before you show up, but I was feeling good, and it was a nearby call, and money is money, so I jumped it.

The fare turned out to be a construction worker whose car had broken down on the way to work and he had been trying to catch a ride for three hours. I won't bore you with his sob story the way he bored me, but after I dropped him off at his construction site, another call came over the radio for a fare that was one block away. I jumped it immediately. That's the ideal situation for a cab driver. It's like playing pool. You try to position yourself every time you drop off a fare so you can pick up a nearby fare. I was sinking shots left and right that day, baby.

The fare turned out to be a young businessman who needed a ride down to the Denver Technical Center, which is a massive business park south of the city. Young businessmen are my favorite customers, turks with the facts and figures at their fingertips, men on the make in their five-hundred-dollar suits and forty-dollar haircuts. Well-bred, intelligent, articulate—even in conversations with me they talk as though they're making a presentation at a board meeting. They always seem curious about my job, the gut details, how much mileage do I rack up in a year, and are the old Checker cabs still being manufactured? It's a treat to talk to junior executives. I imagine how easily they would finesse me in business deals if I was one of their kind. Strategies, stats, game plans, they thrive on the very things that stump me.

But this guy was different. He was probably ten years younger than me, and had an air of smugness about him. I didn't blame him. He was wearing a suit. I once had a suit, and a job to go with it. I felt pretty smug on my first day at the office. The smugness lasted an hour. The job lasted a year. It was at a corporation called Dyna-Plex. It's also located at the "Tech Center" as we Denverites call it. Denverites love to say "Tech Center." Sometimes we shorten it even further to "DTC." It's kind of like saying "LoDo," meaning "Lower Downtown Denver," but let's move on.

He asked me the usual questions about cab driving, how long I had been doing it, was it dangerous, had I ever been robbed, etc. Standard fare chatter. But then, when we were about five minutes away from the Tech Center he said, "Do you plan on doing this all your life?"

I glanced in the rear-view mirror.

Did I mention that he had a briefcase? It was upright on his lap. He was holding it by the handle, utilizing both hands. I could tell he liked his briefcase. It was leather bound. I could smell it.

"I rarely make plans," I said.

"Seems to me you could do better than this," he said.

I interpreted his statement to mean that I ought to be doing what he was doing, whatever that was—being a success or something. He was young. Maybe he wanted me to start asking him questions about his job. Perhaps he wanted to talk about himself and do a little bragging, or "tooting his own horn," as me ol' Dad used to say. I usually cut young people a lot of slack. I know how gauche the young can be, and early success can go to your head, so I've been told. Never been there.

I thought about telling him that I planned on making a fortune writing bestsellers, but decided against it. He might ask me to explain precisely how I intended to go about bringing this grandiose plan to fruition, and I had enough problems fleshing out the subtle details of my fantasy without wrestling with the nuances of reality.

"I'm not qualified to do much of anything else," I said.

"What are the qualifications to drive a cab?" he said in a tone of voice that I can only describe as "supercilious."

"To tell you the truth, there aren't all that many qualifications," I said. "Mostly you need a clean motor-vehicle record. But there is a catch."

"What's that?"

"Catch-23."

"What do you mean?"

"Anyone who has a desire to drive a cab is considered insane, so he isn't allowed to drive a cab."

He frowned, then leaned toward me. "I'm not sure I understand. Are you telling me that only people who don't want to drive cabs are allowed to drive?"

"That's correct."

"But … why would anybody become a cab driver if he didn't want to drive a cab?"

"Catch-24," I said, as I wheeled into the Tech Center and began heading toward his office.

"What's that?"

"Anybody who does something he doesn't want to do is considered insane, so he's forbidden to drive a cab."

He sat back in his seat and thought this over. "Well … by that logic, there shouldn't be any cab drivers at all."

"Catch-25," I said, as I pulled up at the entrance to his building.

"You're not making any sense," he said as he pulled out his wallet.

"Catch-26," I said.

"Keep the change," he said, dropping two tens onto the front seat.

"Catch-27."

He got out and slammed the door shut and walked away.

I always pull that schtick on people who look down on cab driving. It gives them something to be irritated about for the rest of their lives.

I pulled away from the building and drove down the block until I came within sight of the hi-rise Dyna-Plex building. It looked exactly like it had on the day I quit my old job. I wondered who was doing my job now. My job had been to write twelve brochures a year, which meant I worked twelve hours a year.

Just for kicks I tried to work up some nostalgia for the old place, but all it did was make me want to smoke a cigarette. I decided to get the hell out of there.

I took I-25 north toward downtown Denver, listening for calls on the radio. I hated to deadhead for such a long distance, but I wasn't about to hang out at one of the Tech Center hotels. The fares from the DTC hotels are good but the lines are too long for me. The DTC cabstands are similar to DIA, except you don't have to wait three hours for a trip, although that can happen. It's a gamble. I always leave gambling up to the bright-eyed newbies looking for a big score, although I do know old pros who work the Tech Center on a regular basis. But each to his own, I always say. I have smaller fish to fry. I conquered the dream of the big score a long time ago, as far as cab driving goes. I save my big dream for the typewriter, but let's not get into that.

I had just come off I-25 at Lincoln Street when a call came over the radio. The address was in central downtown. I grabbed it because the long drive from the Tech Center had left a bad taste in my mouth. Deadheading will do that, and I wanted to get back into the game. The dispatcher gave me an address that I recognized, then he said something that made me wish I hadn't jumped the bell: "Party named Trowbridge. He'll be waiting outside."

CHAPTER 4

See? This is what I meant when I said that in the world of cab driving, everything evens out. I had been doing well that afternoon, banking balls off bumpers and sinking every shot, but now I was behind the eight ball again. The mover was back: Trowbridge. I continued up Lincoln filled with bitterness. I had given up on the dream of scoring big long ago, but it still scalded my ass to get roped into what amounted to a repeat short trip. I didn't have any doubt about it. The worst part was knowing it ahead of time—another half-hour shot to hell. The fact that I sometimes spent an entire hour seated in a cab line outside a hotel reading a paperback and sipping a Coke without a care in the world did nothing to lessen my irritation. Einstein was right when he blew the lid off relativity.

I saw Trowbridge as soon as I came around the corner. He was standing at the curb wearing the same shabby clown suit, but there weren't as many boxes laid at his feet. I knew where they were, though: inside the building. Doubtless he was playing a game. He wouldn't want to scare off a cabbie by displaying a vast array of personal belongings out front.

Let me tell you a truth about taxi driving: cabbies do not have to pick up anybody that they really don't want to pick up. If a cab driver feels that the impending fare might be dangerous, he can bypass him as long as he lets the dispatcher know about it. People have funny ideas about cab drivers and cab rules. For instance, people think that if they call a taxi company and request service, the company "sends" a cab driver to their address, as if we cabbies hung around an office waiting to be "sent"

somewhere. Not true. Cab driving is one of the last bastions of free enterprise, and when a civilian calls a cab company, the dispatcher hollers
the address over the radio and any driver who wants the trip can claim it,
but if no driver does, then the civilian is out of luck.

By out of luck I mean that the civilian has to take a bus, or walk, or
call his cranky buddy who owns a car. Civilians don't always understand
this. They don't understand why cabs sometimes never arrive at their
homes, especially when the weather is bad. If it's snowing and you're trying to get home from a grocery store with a cart full of plastic bags, good
luck, because all the cabbies are hauling rich people to the airport. I don't
know why I'm telling you this. Cab companies like to keep this info on
the QT. I'll probably get canned now.

Trowbridge gave a little flip of his hand as I pulled up to the curb.
Same procedure as last time. I won't bore you with the details, except to
say that I was curious to see if he would recognize me. He didn't indicate
it, but then he didn't look at me very closely. I got out and opened the
trunk, and he dumped his worldly possessions next to my spare tire.
Then he headed for the right rear door of 127. This surprised me.

"Is that everything for the trunk?" I said.

He glanced back and nodded quickly, then climbed into the backseat.

The guy didn't have as many worldly possessions today. This made
me feel bad. I wondered if he had been forced to hock some of them.
But it was none of my business. Frankly I was pleased, because it short-
ened the length of my downtime. My bitterness had been wasted. This
was turning out to be a regular fare. He gave me an address on Capitol
Hill less than five minutes away, near Washington Street and east 19th
Avenue. So I was glad after all that it was a short trip. Get him in and
get him out. That's the number one rule-of-thumb in cab driving. You
automatically make a dollar-fifty as soon as someone climbs into your
taxi and you drop your flag and start your meter. If you do that ten times
a day, your gas and Twinkies are paid in full.

I glanced in my rear-view mirror as I drove toward The Hill. I tried not to be obvious. I tried to make it look like I was just checking to see the traffic behind me, which I rarely do—anybody fool enough to get behind my taxi is living dangerously. But I was really examining Trowbridge. He looked morose. He was sitting slouched, gazing out the side window. I thought about telling him that I had picked him up a few days earlier, but I didn't want to embarrass him. I only embarrass people who enjoy a higher income-bracket than myself. That includes practically everybody in North America, but Trowbridge wasn't one of them. I don't claim to be a fount of wisdom, but I know a doppelganger when I see one.

The address wasn't far from the site of the old Fern Hill bookstore. I know all the used bookstores in Denver. They come and go, thrive and die. Fern Hill is gone now, but I used to shop there when I first came to Denver. I collect old paperbacks. Next to watching TV, my favorite thing to do at home besides sleeping is browsing through my collection of vintage potboilers. It's kind of like being a model-railroading buff. 'Nuff said on that subject, hey?

I had to parallel park because the street was narrow and there was traffic. Like most cab drivers, I hate to parallel park at a curb. You may have had experience in your lifetime with the infamous "double-parked taxi." It might even have been me. I'll admit it. I do it. I won't make excuses. I double-park whenever I can. Being a cab driver is like being a drunk—you've always got an excuse for everything. The excuse for double-parking is: "I'm trying to make a living here, give me a break!" I could offer more colorful variations, but the First Amendment is not a license to shock old ladies.

By the time I got parked, Trowbridge already had his billfold out. He handed me a five and said, "Keep it," then opened his door. I stuffed the bill into my T-shirt pocket and hopped out to open the trunk for him.

He gathered his boxes and set them on the sidewalk, and I thumped the lid closed. "Need any help carrying your things inside?" I said, but he just shook his head no. Didn't even look at me. I could tell he was embarrassed, but his embarrassment seemed to have diminished in direct proportion to his worldly belongings, which had been halved. I didn't stick around to add to his mortification. I only do that to my friends.

I got back into 127, started the engine, and pulled away. I glanced at my rear-view mirror and saw Trowbridge trundling his boxes up to the door of the apartment building. The whole trip had taken less than ten minutes. I figured if I could get a steady flow of trips like that, I could make thirty bucks an hour. This is how cab drivers think. Even after you've abandoned the dream of the big score, you still waste your time making nonsensical calculations. It's a PUC regulation.

I headed back down The Hill and decided to make a run past the Brown Palace to see how long the line at the cabstand was. The Brown Palace is my favorite hotel to wait outside while reading paperbacks and eating Twinkies. It's an historic hotel, and I do like Denver history. I don't know why the word "historic" has to have the word "an" in front of it. This isn't England, fer the luvva Christ. But that's what they taught us at UCD, and I'm not about to argue with English professors. I gave up on that when I was a student and told a professor that the word "English" itself is misspelled. I told him it ought to be spelled "Anglish," since the language is named after the Angles. I don't know where the Jutes and Saxons fit in, but I do know this: the sonofabitch Anglish professor gave me a C- for the semester.

There were only three cabs at the Brown, so I parked at the rear of the line. It was time to pull a little first-echelon maintenance on my trip-sheet, the dullest part of cab driving. The dullest part of life, too, I suppose—paperwork. I began writing down all the starting points and drop-off points of my morning's fares, and roughly estimating the times of departure and arrival. This is my favorite part of doing paperwork: lying. It sort of reminds me of April 15. Not that I cheat on my income taxes. I don't earn enough money to cheat on my taxes, although I hope to eventually take part in that national pastime. I sometimes feel like such an outsider.

I plucked my money from my shirt pocket in order to sort it out and hide the twenties in a place that I won't reveal to you, although it was not on my physical person. That's when I noticed the handwriting on the fiver that Trowbridge had given to me.

I froze.

The writing was in tiny print along the top edge where the paper is greenish-white. It looked like a punch line coming out of Abraham Lincoln's mouth. He was saying, "You must harbor a secret in your past so dreadful and shameful that the mere thought of it sends you lurching violently to the nearest liquor store."

The cramped, squared printing was the same as the printing on the other fiver stuck in my Camus back home, so I was certain that Trowbridge had written it. But I didn't know why.

My paranoia began to well up. This was not unusual. In fact I would say it was overdue for the day. I glanced at my wristwatch. It was getting on toward three in the afternoon. Yep—if I'm not stricken by a nauseating wave of paranoia by lunchtime, I start to get worried.

But this was different. Most of my paranoia is generated by what my Maw used to call my "active imagination," meaning that it was all in my mind and really had nothing to do with the dirty looks given to me by friends, nuns, clerks, cops, and taxi fares after having innocently said something that they may or may not have taken offense at. You might not believe this, but I often say things that I regret. But I had never actually held in my hands a manifest cause for paranoia.

I stared at the message coming from ol' Honest Abe's face, and again noted the word "must" tucked between the words "You" and "harbor." It possessed the definite quality of a command, not a mere suggestion or observation. The fact that I do harbor shameful secrets in my past made me feel like I was seated naked inside my taxi. That guy Trowbridge seemed to have me pegged, because one of my shameful secrets involves sitting naked inside a taxi. That was back in college. It was during Spring-time Crazy Days at Wichita State University, an annual celebration that takes place each March prior to spring break. I won't bore you with the details of how I ended up naked inside a taxi in the middle of downtown Wichita. Let's just say it involved a streaking incident combined with the misreading of a street sign, plus quite a bit of beer.

At any rate, I decided to separate the fiver from the rest of my daily take. I knew what I was going to do with it and knew exactly where it belonged: in between the pages of Albert Camus' *L'Étranger*, the foun-tainhead of absurd human behavior and the graveyard where all mysteries go to die.

CHAPTER 5

I tried to put the fiver out of my mind as I drove the remainder of my shift, but that was like trying to forget my first kiss. With a girl I mean, not "of death."

I've always thought of a high school diploma as the first kiss of death because it means you have to go out and get a job, or at least start making adult decisions—unless you plan to go to college. I highly recommend college to any young person who has no active interest in adulthood. Unfortunately college costs quite a bit of money nowadays, so unless you want to get a job to pay your way through college—which completely nullifies the whole point of going to college—you might have to trick your parents into thinking you want to become a doctor or a lawyer or an engineer. This might motivate them to pay your expenses. Your parents might even "get the impression" that you intend to pay them back someday—if you get my drift.

I myself wasn't fortunate enough to be born into a family of dupes. If I had tried to convince my Maw that I wanted to become an M.D., LL.D., or a bridge builder, she would have dragged me to confession and made me beg absolution for violating the Sixth Commandment and any other Roman numeral she could think of. My decision not to take that dangerous fork in the road may have been the first adult decision I ever made in my life. Instead, I got drafted. And let me tell you, two years in the army was almost as bad as two minutes in the confessional with Monsignor O'Leary. But after I got out, the GI Bill gave me enough money to go to college for four years—seven if you did it my way, but let's not get into that.

I completed my shift for the day and drove home slightly chagrined by the fact that I had earned only forty-five dollars rather than my minimum fifty. I couldn't bring myself to include the Trowbridge fiver in the total, even though I knew the day would come when I would spend it, along with the crispy in my Camus, probably on a Saturday night when I was low on beer and the liquor store down the block was five minutes from closing—i.e., the following Saturday night.

When I got home I climbed the fire escape to my crow's nest, dropped my cab accouterment on the kitchen table, and headed for my bookshelves. I plugged my daily take into the *Finnegans*, then pulled out *The Stranger* and opened it. Before I put the second fiver into the book I reread the hand printing: "You must harbor a secret in your past so dreadful and shameful that the mere thought of it sends you lurching violently to the nearest liquor store."

Pegged.

But assuming he wasn't referring to me, why would anyone write down such a peculiar statement? What was it that drove Trowbridge not just to print words on American currency, but to write anything at all? I had been writing unpublished novels since I was in college, and I knew exactly what drove me to do it: money. But why would anybody write for free? Why would anybody write at all if they didn't have to?

I was amazed whenever I met students in creative writing classes in college who had no intention of going on to become professional fiction writers. What the hell were they doing in creative writing classes? Seeking self-fulfillment? They could do that kicking a hacky sack. Years later it occurred to me that they might have been lying, and that they actually intended to try and become novelists, but they just wouldn't admit it. After all, if you tried to become a novelist and failed, people might laugh at you. I've been there. I'm still there.

I took one last look at the crispy, then stuffed it into my Camus. One thing that struck me about the handwriting was that it reminded me of

William Faulkner's handwriting. I don't mean the "content" of the message, but the printing itself. I once saw a sample of William Faulkner's handwriting.

This was at a book fair held at Currigan Hall in midtown a few years ago. Being a book lover and a collector of paperbacks, I had decided to go to the fair on the off-chance that I might find something that not only would be unique but that I might be able to afford. But first let me explain something to you about book collecting.

I like to find my vintage potboilers at flea markets and used bookstores, preferably stores run by people who don't know what they're doing. These types of bookstores might be run by, for example, little old ladies who specialize in bodice rippers but who occasionally receive vintage paperbacks that have no cachet with the frustrated housewives who buy Harlequin romances by the bucketful. The owners often put the vintage books on obscure racks at the backs of their stores rather than throw them away. I love those little old ladies. They cannot bring themselves to toss the printed word into the trash, yet at the same time they have no hope that they will ever sell the books. But they do. They sell them to me.

I own a number of mint condition, first edition paperbacks written by Jack Kerouac, thanks to those ladies. I cannot begin to tell you how my heart throbs every time I walk into a store filled with romance novels. My only fear is that someday all the other Kerouac fans in Denver will learn this secret. I have also found other treasures, such as my French version of *The Plague* by Albert Camus published in 1947. It's printed in French and titled *La Peste*. On the back cover is a picture of Albert himself with a cigarette dangling from his lips. He looks like Jean Paul Belmondo's black-sheep cousin.

But buying a vintage paperback at a book fair?

Well ... that has the taint of cheating. Anybody with the bucks could scout out and buy a complete set of autographed Kerouacs if he felt like it.

So obviously it's not just the books themselves, but the thrill of the hunt that appeals to me when it comes to collecting. Whenever I find a first edition paperback that's worth more than the twenty-five cents demanded by a flea-market proprietor, I feel like a crazed sourdough who has just discovered the Dutchman's lost goldmine. Fantasy role-playing consumes a large chunk of my life. It's right up there with denial and television.

But back to William Faulkner. At the Currigan fair I came across a hardback copy of *Pylon* by Faulkner which was part of a limited printing of numbered and signed editions. The proprietor allowed me to open the book, and there was William Faulkner's signature in the tiniest cramped printing I had ever seen in my life, until I met Trowbridge. I'll admit it. It gave me a thrill to be holding a book once held by the man from Mississippi. I'm only human. Fame does the same thing to me that it does to Elvis nuts. Then the proprietor told me the book was priced at one hundred dollars. I closed the book and handed it back.

A few years later I mentioned this incident to a rare-book dealer who told me that I ought to have bought the Faulkner. "You can add a zero to that price today," he said. Then he showed me a literary Blue Book that gave current prices for rare editions. The autographed *Pylon* was listed at more than a thousand dollars.

I can't go on with that story.

I walked into the kitchen and cooked up a hamburger. While it was frying I grabbed a beer from the fridge and sipped at it and pretended that I wasn't going to think anymore about Trowbridge and his money messages. I wandered into the living room and picked up the TV schedule and began checking out the stations with reruns of *Gilligan's Island*. As it turned out I would be eating my dinner during what I call "The Black Hole," meaning there was an hour during which no Gilligan'ses were being shown either in Denver or in any of our video sister cities such as Chicago, New York, or Los Angeles. I would have to settle for the lesser classics of television, like Dick Van Dyke or Andy of Mayberry, not that

I have anything against those shows. In my opinion, Barney Fife is the greatest character ever created for television. But he's no Mary Ann. Just the thought of Don Knotts wearing tight denim short-shorts is enough to put me off my feed.

But I was just kidding myself. I couldn't get Trowbridge out of my mind. Why did he write those things? Were they instructions to himself? Or were they merely observations about himself? I was willing to dismiss the idea that he was making observations about me. I've been around my paranoia long enough to ignore it, although that's like trying to ignore a small dog known to bite.

When I was a kid living in Wichita, our family owned a sheltie dog. She was a psychotic little bitch. You could feed her a steak dinner, and ten minutes later you could look at her cross-eyed and she would go for your ankles. I'll admit it. Me and Gavin used to look at her cross-eyed on purpose, but we explained to our Maw that we did it just to disprove the theory that "a dog will not bite the hand that feeds it." My brother and I liked to pretend we were scientists, but we were just jerks. The sheltie's name was "Shelteen." My sisters named her of course.

After I finished my burger I did the dish, then went into the living room and stood looking at the bookshelf. I have some bookshelves in my apartment that are built out of old novel manuscripts. The rest are brick and plank, the way hippies and broke people do it. I've written a lot of novels since I was in college, but I use only manuscripts that have absolutely no hope of ever being published to build the bookshelves. I use them in place of the bricks. Admittedly, bookshelves made out of paper are not the most structurally sound things on earth, but neither are my novels.

As I stood there staring at the Trowbridge vault, it occurred to me that it had been a long time since I had attempted to write a novel. I used to write screenplays, but I had given up on that after I realized I didn't have what it took to write movies. I know that sounds like a crazy reason to give up on screenplays, but it's not as crazy as my reason for trying to write them in the first place, which was to make some quick money to support me while I wrote novels. Don't get me started on convoluted logic.

But those two little missives from Trowbridge had gotten me to thinking about starting a new novel, had put me "in the mood." Maybe it was seeing somebody else do some actual writing that bent my twig in that direction, or maybe it was the cosmic combination of words and money, but I could feel the itch to drag my Smith Corona out and start putting words on paper.

The desire to write is one of the few desires I possess that doesn't overwhelm me in the way that the desire to drink beer or smoke cigars does. Or watch TV. Or date. Or sleep till noon. I'm not that good at resisting desires, but for some reason I'm able to fend off my desire to write. Sounds inconsistent if not completely illogical I know, but there you have it.

In the end though, it was the thought of going all the way across the room to my closet, and reaching up for my typewriter on the top shelf, that took the wind out of my sails. It was just too much trouble. I figured what I ought to do was wait until the weekend, when I wasn't so tired from sitting all day in my taxi, and had the energy to open my closet door and retrieve the Smith Corona and set it on my beer table next to my easy chair. By doing this, I would be prepared, should the urge to write well up inside me again.

I wonder where the phrase "well up" came from. Did wells used to overflow a lot in Angland?

Anyway, this seemed like such a good plan that I decided to make a note of it and post it on my bulletin board in the kitchen as a reminder. But after searching all over my apartment for half an hour I couldn't find any yellow stickies, so I gave up the whole scheme and finished off my beer, went into the bedroom, kicked off my Keds, and collapsed into bed.

CHAPTER 6

It was Monday. I always feel especially decadent on Monday because of the two-day weekend break from driving. I also take Tuesday and Thursday off during the weeks when I'm not hard up for dough—meaning when I don't have to make the rent on my crow's nest. Having one day off twice a week "feels just right" if you know what I mean, but the two-day weekend makes me feel like Caligula. It "feels just right," too, in its own way, but I'm always eager to get back on the road when Monday comes. I never would have believed I would look forward to working, but since taxi driving is legally defined as "work" by the State of Colorado, I guess that makes me a hypocrite.

I've never liked any job as much as I like cab driving. I've never liked any other job at all, frankly, and I've done a lot of jobs in a lot of cities, from Pittsburgh to Los Angeles, from delivering handbills to delivering sofa beds. I washed dishes in Kansas City and mopped floors in a medical clinic in San Francisco, and I hated every single second of my life during those years. The day part I mean. Not the TV or bar part. So cab driving means a lot to me. Sometimes when I drive I feel like one of those gleeful singers or comics you see on TV who say, "I can't believe they pay me to do this." That makes two of us, pal.

But I've always suspected that if I ever won a million dollars in the lottery I wouldn't feel any different than I do now, meaning I would still go on feeling like I didn't have a care in the world. This is pure speculation on my part of course, since I have no idea what it actually feels like to be a millionaire. Never been there. Hope to get there. Trying hard. Buck a day. That's the amount I spend on lottery tickets when I'm driving.

I figure what the hell, blowing three dollars a week on the chance that I might become filthy rich is a bargain—only in America, huh? And Canada. Also Asia, Mexico, and Europe, but what I'm getting at is that during the past fourteen years I've never given any serious thought to doing anything else besides driving a cab. I wouldn't know what to do if for some reason the human race decided it didn't need lackeys. Believe me, I don't lose any sleep over that.

So I was feeling pretty good when I woke up on Monday and headed out to Rocky Cab, which is located near the I-70 viaduct north of the city. If you've ever driven Interstate 70 across Denver, then you've been in what the police refer to as "the immediate vicinity" of my place of employment. Back in 1978, a semi tractor-trailer went off the viaduct and landed in a vacant lot half a block from Rocky Cab. I don't know why I bring that up, except it's kind of a legend around the motor. Stew would be glad to fill you in on the details. You can still see the axles.

I walked into the on-call room at Rocky that morning and picked up the keys to 127. The cage man, Rollo, was too busy handing out trip-sheets to give me more than a perfunctory snub. Everybody was working that day, newbies and old pros. Mondays are good taxi days. Businessmen are flying into DIA, and hotels are kicking out the weekend guests. We cabbies refer to Monday as "Little Friday" since Friday is the busiest day of all for cabbies.

I went out to the parking lot and checked 127 for dents and dings but didn't find any. I checked the oil, water, and air, then hopped in and drove out of the lot. I radioed the dispatcher that I was on the road, and I headed for a nearby 7-11 where I gassed up and bought a package of Twinkies. As I said earlier, this was how my life had been going for the past couple of months—"smooth sailing" as the creative writing teachers tell you not to say.

I headed for the Brown Palace Hotel and found only one taxi ahead of me in line, a Yellow Cab who nabbed a passenger coming out the front door as soon as I pulled up behind him. This annoyed me. As much as I like making money hand-over-fist, I like taking a half hour at dawn to eat my Twinkies in peace and read a few pages of a paperback before diving into the asphalt fray. Since I know I'm going to earn only fifty bucks for the day, I see no reason to get excited. In fact, I feel rather put upon when I drive up to a hotel and don't have time to turn off my engine. In this way I am different from every other cab driver I know, with the exception of Big Al, who trained me to drive a taxi fourteen years ago.

Big Al possesses more or less the same attitude that I do, in that he knows you cannot win in this game, meaning you will never earn The Big Money. Just as my Big Dream involves the writing of bestsellers, his Big Dream involves winning at the dogs and the horses, although he tends to get more acceptance slips than I do. I tend to get zero. Big Al also knows exactly how much taxi money he is going to earn each day: one hundred dollars. For you non-math majors out there, that's twice the money I earn. From a mathematical standpoint this makes perfect sense because he works twice as hard as I do, although he would submit that I work half as hard as he does.

My first score of the day came out five minutes after I parked. It was two men in suits. I had just finished swallowing my last Twinkie but was still savoring the flavor, so it put a damper on my brunch. But I swallowed a quick gulp of Coke and waited for my fares to climb in. They were not hauling luggage. This was a bad sign. It meant they were not going to DIA.

"DIA," one of them said as they got settled in the backseat. Live and learn.

But this made me feel good. Just the fact that I didn't have to spend forty-seven seconds putting things into the trunk, and then repeating the process at the airport, made me forget the Twinkie debacle. Forty-seven seconds is the average amount of time I spend outside my taxi per trip. I had made a scientific study of this. It took fourteen years and three wristwatches.

As I pulled away from the Brown and headed toward 17th Avenue to work my way over to I-70, I casually said, "How are you doing today?"

Note that I used the plural "you." The Anglish language doesn't have a fancy plural personal pronoun for "you" like the Romance languages do—it has to be gleaned from the context, but they got it.

"We're fine, thank you," one of them said.

I quickly ran his tone through my mental Univac, and it spit out a card that told me to back off. Things weren't fine at all. I recognized it. Every now and then I get a sad businessman in my taxi. After fourteen years my Univac is attuned to the nuances of business deals gone sour. I quickly turned on the Rocky radio so the cab would be filled with some noise, although I kept the dispatcher's voice low. This was "official" noise that created a psychological wall between myself and the businessmen, which I knew they would want. They were not up to inane chatter that day. This was confirmed when I heard one of them sigh and say, "I'll call Hudspeth when we get back to Detroit."

The other man said nothing, but I saw the brief movement of a sad nod in my rear-view mirror. Yep. Hudspeth was not going to be happy with the news, whatever it was. I always feel bad when businessmen fail. Another "Big Carruthers Deal" had not panned out. This is a code name for failed business deals that I coined to myself twelve years back when two businessmen climbed into my taxi and one of them remarked to the other that the big Carruthers deal had not panned out. The man said it in a melancholy tone of voice. I didn't need my Univac to interpret it. I know melancholy when I hear it. Sooner or later, in everybody's life, the Big Carruthers Deal doesn't pan out. It's like the time back in Wichita when I was in college and I asked Mary Margaret Flaherty to marry me. The Big Carruthers Deal didn't pan out.

When we arrived at the airport I did something I occasionally do to make people feel better. I offered both of them a receipt. The Rocky Cab receipt is a 2x3-inch card that tells the time and date and cost of a trip, which I sign and give to a fare at the end of the ride. The fare, usually a businessman, theoretically turns the card over to the accounting department at his company so he can be reimbursed for the cost of the trip. The cabbie is supposed to give only one receipt per trip, and the cabbie is supposed to sign and fill out the cost himself. But sometimes I remember only to sign it. I'm a pretty busy guy, so I don't always have time to fill out the cost of the ride. I just let my fare fill in the dollar amount at his leisure, if you get my drift.

So when I held out the two signed receipts to the businessmen they brightened up a bit. Maybe the Big Carruthers Deal had fallen through for them, but the Little Murph Deal is as good as gold in any accounting department in America. They each tipped me an extra five bucks.

I deadheaded out of DIA after that. I didn't bother to cruise past the staging area to see if by some miracle the cab line was short. It was Monday morning, meaning the line might be moving faster than normal, meaning a two-hour wait instead of a three-hour wait, but I wasn't in the mood to sit still for two hours. I figure that a smart movie mogul could pick up a few extra bucks erecting a drive-in theater screen at the taxi stand at DIA.

I deadheaded back toward downtown, listening to the dispatcher yell at the newbies, and keeping an ear open for any bells that might come up in the vicinity of my cab. Maybe that construction worker would need another lift to the site. This is the kind of thought that cabbies have, hoping for a repeat performance of a run of good luck. I understand that gamblers at craps tables have the same futile hopes. Never been there. Never plan to go there. The truth is, I'm afraid to learn how to play craps. I figure I'm the personality type who would learn just enough to get really bad at it. Sort of like writing novels, but more expensive.

Then an address that I recognized came over the radio. It was on east 19th Avenue. I knew who it was. I didn't jump it. I kept driving. I kept waiting to hear another cabbie snatch the call. Nobody took it. The dispatcher went on with other bells and other addresses, then came back and offered the east 19th Avenue again. I wondered what the hell was wrong with all the other Rocky drivers. Hey! Free money on Capitol Hill! What's the matter with you idiots!

The only conceivable explanation was that they were too busy, or else snoozing at the hotels and didn't want to be bothered with a Hill run. The truth is, only a handful of drivers work The Hill on any given day. Usually old pros, or else starry-eyed newbies who will take anything. The old pros are guys willing to make short runs all day long. The fares are small but they add up. It's the kind of work that I call "hard." I sort of fall somewhere between starry-eyed and old, in that I want lengthy trips in between snoozes. At any rate, nobody was jumping what I knew was a Trowbridge call.

All of a sudden I started feeling sorry for Trowbridge. He was probably waiting outside his latest awful digs looking up and down the street for his Rocky Cab. It made me think of The Little Match Girl. Also the girl in that song by Bobby Darin, "Artificial Flowers." I'll admit it. I like corn. I own a Glenn Miller album if you want to know the truth. Anyway, I finally snatched up the mike and took the bell. The fact is, I wanted the bell. I wanted to know if Trowbridge would hand me another Lincoln log … and at the same time I didn't want to know. Kind of like a little kid who wants to ride a roller coaster, but at the same time he doesn't. His friends finally resort to ridicule to make him get on the Cyclone. I was ten years old. They called me "chicken," but let's move on.

Trowbridge was standing outside the building with even fewer personal possessions than before, but at least he was wearing clothes. That's more than I was wearing during Crazy Days.

I didn't even have to open the trunk for him. But I did hop out to open the right rear door. He picked up two small boxes bulging with his stuff and mumbled "Thank you," then climbed into the backseat. I felt bad for him as I rounded the cab and climbed in.

"Where to?' I said, glancing in my rear-view mirror. Trowbridge raised his chin and looked at me, then looked out the front window. He didn't answer. I started the engine, took hold of the gearshift, then glanced back to sort of encourage him to speak. That's an old cabbie trick.

But he just kept staring out the front window. My cab was facing west, and he seemed to be gazing at the range of the Rocky Mountains in the distance. I began to grow wary. Silence in a taxi can be unnerving. It can even be a preamble to a stickup under the wrong circumstances. I finally hoisted myself around and looked him in the eye. He was holding the boxes on his lap. He was sort of clutching them.

"Where ya headed?" I said in a jovial tone of voice. Joviality is another old cabbie trick, but I hate to employ it because it makes me feel like a transparent phony.

"Buffalo Bill's grave," he said.

Now the silence came from me. I stared at him, but he wasn't looking at me, he was looking at the Rockies.

"What do you mean?" I said.

He finally turned his gaze toward me. "Lookout Mountain," he said.

"You want to go up Lookout Mountain?" I said.

He nodded. "Buffalo Bill is buried up there. They have a museum and a gift shop that I'd like to visit."

Lookout Mountain stands at the edge of the foothills west of Denver. At the base of the mountain is a town called Golden. You have to pass through Golden to get to the top of the mountain. According to legend, Lookout Mountain was where William "Buffalo Bill" Cody sat on his horse during the nineteenth century and looked for buffalo out on the plains. But I had my doubts about that legend. Getting to the top of the mountain by car took long enough. If you went up there on a horse and happened to spot any buffalo, it would take forever to get back down. By then the buffalo would be gone. In fact the buffalo are gone.

I frowned and kept my hand away from the gearshift. It could be an hour's drive from Capitol Hill to the top of Lookout Mountain, and I wasn't confident that Trowbridge had the money to pay for the ride. The proper course to follow in a dicey situation like this is to ask the fare to show you the money first. This isn't an old cabbie trick. It's an old desperation move. You can easily get stiffed on a long ride. A cabbie has to take a number of things into consideration when a fare requests a long trip, and one of the things that you base your judgment on is the clothing the fare is wearing. If he doesn't look like he can afford a shoeshine, you ask him to show you the money first, which can be awkward, embarrassing, and profitable.

But I couldn't bring myself to do it. I thought about those fivers he had been spreading all over town, and I suddenly wondered if he was a counterfeiter. This made me decide to take the risk. Cab driving is a risky business. Life is a risky business. But if he was a counterfeiter, he was probably loaded with rubber dough that could be laundered fast. There were plenty of car-wash change machines that took five-dollar bills. Clean and simple—no fingerprints. I would make sure of that. I had seen plenty of cop shows.

CHAPTER 7

I headed down The Hill and stopped behind a bus waiting for a red light at Lincoln Street. "There's a couple of routes to Golden," I said. "We could take Sixth Avenue, or else head out Interstate 70 and take the 58th Avenue exit. Depends on how fast you want to get there."

I always give the customers an option if I can. I want them out of my cab as quickly as possible because, as I said, I score a buck-fifty with every new fare. But Golden is fifteen miles from Denver so either route was fine with me. We were at a kind of fork in the road, although I-70 might have added a couple bucks to the meter, but believe it or not I was indifferent. Sergeant Bilko said it best: You'll Never Get Rich. Speed was my main concern.

But Trowbridge didn't answer right away. I gritted my teeth and waited. It was going to be one of "those" trips.

Then he said, "If you don't mind, I'd like to take Forty-fourth Avenue out to Golden."

My heart sank. That was the slowest route he could have picked. "Forty-fourth?" I said. "Are you sure?"

"Yes," he said. "I grew up in Wheatridge and I'd like to take a look at … my old stomping grounds."

My heart kept sinking but my Univac went into high gear. I had to calculate the fastest route along the slowest route in town. Broadway to 23rd to Fox to 38th, and then hopefully clear past Wadsworth Boulevard with no sightseeing side trips. I was already immersed in regret. Why couldn't I have left it alone?

Why couldn't I have stayed away from Capitol Hill? Why did I have to … get involved in … the personal …

I couldn't bring myself to finish the thought.

I had made a vow long ago to never again get involved in the personal lives of my fares, and yet here I was, like a moth to a flame, like a child to an orange—I had actually gone out of my way to pick up Trowbridge just because I felt sorry for him. What in the hell was wrong with me? I blamed my faulty Univac.

The light turned green. I made a right and worked my way over to the viaduct that would take us across the valley where I-25 and the Platte River runs. The traffic was flying on I-25. I could have been on I-70 within a minute and heading west toward Golden, but instead I found myself waiting for a red light at Fox Street near 38th Avenue. I had blown it. Why had I offered him an option?

One thing I have learned about customers during the past fourteen years is that they fear cab drivers. By this I mean that most of them live with the assumption that cabbies know what they are doing, that cabbies know the best routes to all points of drop-off in Denver, and to question our wisdom is to cross the line! The rest of the customers think we're taking them on the scenic route. But all of them seem to forget that, because they are footing the bill, the driver is required by PUC regulations to do their bidding. If they want to stop off at a bank or a 7-11, that's their option. We have to do what they want. As long as they maintain proper backseat decorum and adhere to the precepts of civilized behavior, we cabbies are pretty much their mobile slaves. You do get the occasional barbarian in your backseat, but when that happens, all the PUC regulations go right out the door, along with your customer.

After the light turned green I swung up to 38th Avenue and settled in for a long trip west. This required an attitude adjustment on my part. Speed was no longer in the loop. I focused my thoughts on the fact that this would be a moneymaking venture, which I rarely do. As you may have gathered, money has never been foremost in my mind when it comes to almost everything except publishing bestsellers. I know this may sound insane, but keeping my backseat vacant as long as possible is my primary goal as a cab driver. I read an average of two hundred paperbacks per year.

"The old beer warehouse," Trowbridge said softly.

I glanced back, "What's that, sir?"

He tapped on the side window and pointed. "I used to drink beer there when I was a young man."

It was a bar he was referring to, not a storage depot. "The Beer Warehouse," said a sign hanging over the doorway.

"That was back in the days when an eighteen-year-old could get legally drunk," he said.

"Oh yeah," I said, eager to get some kind of conversation going. As I have said, silence in a taxi can be unnerving, and I hadn't yet succumbed to the ploy of turning on the Rocky radio to listen to the dispatcher yelling at newbies. I normally listen to the dispatcher as little as possible when I drive. But right then I wished I had stopped listening to him yesterday.

"It's ironic how nowadays you can go to a war when you're eighteen, but you can't do it drunk," I said, thinking about my own army days. "When I was eighteen you could buy beer, sign contracts, vote, and get drafted, sometimes in the same week."

He nodded. We rode for a few more blocks. "Elitch's is gone," Trowbridge said.

I glanced to my left as we passed the site of the old Elitch's Amusement Park. All the rides had been dismantled and the park had moved to the Platte Valley. I often went to Elitch's when I first came to Denver. One night I rode the roller coaster eight times in a row on purpose. That was the last time I ever did anything on purpose.

"A shame they had to tear it down," he said. "I celebrated my eighth birthday in Kiddieland. All my old friends from the third grade were there. The whole gang."

I glanced in my rear-view mirror. "The theater is still there."

He nodded but didn't say anything. I debated whether or not to tell him that many years ago I had seen Mickey Rooney coming out of the Elitch Theater. I decided not to tell him, but it took an effort. I've told practically everybody I've ever known that I once saw Mickey Rooney in person. Most people find it to be a real conversation killer.

"Turn right on Sheridan," Trowbridge said.

He wasn't afraid of cabbies. I made the turn, which took us to 44th Avenue. After that it would be a straight shot to Buffalo Bill's grave, not counting the winding hairpin road up Lookout Mountain itself.

I swung left onto 44th and headed out.

"Lakeside Speedway," he said as we drove past a vast lot behind a cyclone fence. "I used to attend stock-car races there when I was a teenager. They had a dirt track."

I glanced at the site. The lot is part of the town of Lakeside, which is comprised solely of an amusement park about the same age as Elitch's. Lakeside even has a mayor and a police department. It's the kind of town I would have liked to live in when I was a kid. They don't make towns with roller coasters anymore. I know a lot about Denver history. I once took a local history class at UCD when I was hiding out from the real world, compliments of the GI Bill.

"Lakeside Shopping Center," he said a few blocks farther along. "I worked as a stock boy at Skaggs Drugstore when I was eighteen. My first job." His voice was wistful. He was seeing his old stomping grounds. I glanced in the mirror and tried to judge his age. I didn't like what I saw. The tinted mirror made him look young. I thought about asking where he went to high school and then surreptitiously asking what year he had graduated. But I didn't want to know. I didn't want to find out that this old timer was younger than me.

We passed into the suburb of Wheatridge, a town that had boomed after World War II—a lot of white clapboard shotgun housing as well as one-story blonde brick ranch houses. But that's the history of America itself. I didn't live in suburbs when I was a kid though. Ancient urban residential, that was my Wichita. I could have grown up in the 1920s and wouldn't have known the difference as far as the architecture was concerned. A couple of nuns at Blessed Virgin Catholic Grade School were born in 1890. It gives me the willies to think that I was educated by people who were alive twenty-five years after Lincoln was shot.

We finally passed Wadsworth Boulevard and entered the wilderness that separates Denver from Golden. I gathered from Trowbridge that the landscape hadn't changed much since he was a boy.

"When I was twelve, my chums and I rode our bicycles out to Golden," he said. "We made a day-trip of it. We pedaled our bikes up Lookout Mountain."

I nearly lost control of the cab. "You what!"

"We rode our bikes up Lookout Mountain."

"Why?" I said. I shouldn't have said that. Why do kids do anything? To get away from their parents, of course.

"It was just something to do," he said.

"Did you have ten-speeds?" I said.

"Oh no, just old-fashioned bicycles."

I started to feel faint. The road up Lookout Mountain is at least five miles on a steep grade. I tried to envision a boy making that climb on a bike without a complex system of high and low gears connected to the chain, and I couldn't do it. My imagination could not envision such a madman stunt. I wanted to call Trowbridge a liar, but instead I felt pity for him, or at least the boy he had been. Didn't they have television in those days? Of course they did, even if it was only three channels. I'd been there. Ergo, Trowbridge and his chums must have been truly desperate for entertainment. I whispered a silent prayer of thanks that I had grown up in Kansas. If you've ever seen a basketball court, you've seen Kansas.

Then we entered Golden. It's a pretty town with a lot of trees. During the nineteenth century it was the territorial capital, until the capital was moved to Denver. That's about all I can tell you about Golden. It's jammed up against the base of Lookout Mountain. I made my way to an intersection that led to a two-lane asphalt road that started the winding climb up the hill, and I tried to imagine a group of little boys on old-fashioned bicycles pedaling up the steep road. It sickened me.

Within a few minutes we were high above the town. It's a fast ride in a car. On a bike though …

"How did you do it?" I said.

"Do what?' Trowbridge said.

"Ride a bike up this hill. It feels like a forty-five degree angle."

"The grade is not quite that steep. But we did get off our bikes and walk them part of the way. It was very difficult."

"I'll bet," I said. "How long did it take you to get to the top?"

"Oh, five or six hours."

A kid could watch a lot of cartoons in five or six hours.

I looked at the rising asphalt ahead of me. Just traveling on foot up that road would be hard enough, but shoving the weight of a bicycle … my mind reeled, and ultimately rejected the entire scenario. I decided to stop thinking about it. Instead, I started wondering if my cab would make it up the hill without blowing the goddamn radiator.

We were halfway up the mountain when Trowbridge said, "Could you pull over here?"

There was a hairpin turn up ahead with a pull-off, the kind of scenic view you might see at the Grand Canyon. It had a low wall made of stone, which looked like a WPA project to me. I pulled off to the right and parked the cab.

"This was always a stopping point for us whenever we rode our bikes up here," Trowbridge said. "We would drink soda pops and wait for the laggards."

I turned around in the seat and looked at him. "You mean you rode up this mountain more than once?"

"Oh yes. Two or three times every summer."

I turned away from him and stared at the eastern plains of Colorado. I could see clear across Kansas, all the way to the St. Louis Arch. Okay, I'm kidding about the arch. But that's what it felt like. Two or three times a summer—was he serious? I felt like I was in the presence of Satan.

"Let's climb out and take a look," he said.

"Get thee behind me," I almost said, except he already was.

CHAPTER 8

The air seemed thin, or was it just my imagination? Was it the sight of Golden so tiny and distant below, with the smoggy smudge of Denver far out on the eastern plains? We were only halfway up the mountain, but the distance to the bottom confirmed in my mind the preposterous notion that Buffalo Bill had sat on a horse looking out over the prairies to spot grub on the hoof. I felt like I was in an airplane. I kept inhaling deeply as if expecting the air to escape from the cabin. I hate flying.

Trowbridge walked ahead of me to the low stone wall that formed a U at the very edge of the cliff, which dropped vertically. Buffalo Bill my ass. The wall wasn't one continuous arch but was made of rectangles that had spaces between them, like the parapet on a castle turret where medieval archers would fire flaming arrows at invaders. I stood beside Trowbridge and looked down at the plains, thinking what a double bummer it would be to get shot by an arrow that was on fire. It must have been tough to be a soldier in those days.

Then I began wondering about scenic views. Why would anybody take the time and trouble to drive up to a place like this? All you can do with a scenic view is look at it. You might as well stare at a photograph.

Trowbridge bent at the waist and slapped a palm on a stone rectangle at the apex of the arch. "This is the very spot where I sat," he said. "I always chose this pillar to sit on and drink a can of soda and watch the stragglers pushing their bicycles up the hill."

He smiled. "It was a point of pride for us boys to climb onto our bikes and pedal the last few dozen yards up to where the road levels out here. The more athletic boys always beat me to this place, but I was usually ahead of two or three others. I was kind of a mid-level straggler."

Been there.

He made a slow turn and looked at the other rectangles of stone. But I knew what he was really looking at: the ghosts of all his boyhood chums seated on those artificial stools.

"You asked me a question earlier," Trowbridge said. "And now I remember the answer."

"What question was that?" I said.

"You asked me why we rode our bikes up this mountain."

I nodded.

"The downward journey was so much fun," he said.

He raised his chin and looked to the top of the mountain where the heartwarming silhouettes of television transmission towers rose against the sky. "I had forgotten, but that was our motive. We would ride our bikes all the way to the top of the mountain just so we could experience the thrill of coasting to the bottom without having to pedal once. All you needed was a good set of brakes for the hairpin turns."

He was right. He did answer my question. It needed no further explanation. It made sense to me, more sense even than escaping from parents. A ride down this mountain road on a bicycle just might be worth the effort to pedal to the top. Not to me, but to a normal boy. At last my imagination was able to envision the entire scenario, as ghastly as it appeared on the surface.

"How long did it take to get to the bottom?" I said.

"Oh, fifteen minutes or so."

I inhaled sharply between my teeth. Six hours of hell for fifteen minutes of fun. It was a tough call. But I could see it. I could see young Trowbridge leaning into his handlebars, his hair flying, his heels working the brakes, negotiating the hairpin turns on the wildest ride of his life. But the scenario had the quality of a reverse hangover—first the pain, then the pleasure. I couldn't have done it. I was a lousy boyhood chum.

Trowbridge smiled at me. "One time we asked our parents if they might be willing to load our bikes into the trunks of their cars and drive us to the top of the mountain."

"No go, huh?" I automatically said. I knew parents. I knew how they thought. I had two of them when I was a kid, and two were plenty.

He shook his head no. "We were left to our own devices. It was summer."

I nodded. Parents don't understand summer. They don't understand how to have fun. Parents eat liver fried with onions.

Suddenly I wished I hadn't left the meter running when we had gotten out. Leaving the meter running is a cabbie option. There's no hard and fast rule. It depends on how much money you think you might make. I felt guilty charging Trowbridge for his brief stopover. I thought about sidling back to the cab and shutting it off, but then he said, "See those wrecks down there?" He was pointing straight down the cliff.

I frowned and leaned forward. My hair almost stood on end. A couple hundred yards down the mountainside lay the rusted hulks of ancient automobiles. They were lying crushed up against the trunks of evergreens.

"When I was a boy we always wanted to climb down the cliff and examine the wrecked cars. But that would have meant leaving our bicycles up here. Too risky, although I doubt if many bicycle thieves worked the Lookout Mountain beat."

"Jaysus," I whispered.

"That was our response the first time we saw them. I suppose the highway department built these stone abutments to keep any more accidents from taking place. I would imagine that quite a few careless drivers went off the road before the barriers were erected."

My mind turned away from the sight of the wrecks, and so did my head. But then I had a thought. "Wasn't it dangerous to coast down the road on bicycles?"

"Oh yes," Trowbridge said. "I'm surprised none of us were killed."

Then Trowbridge did something that gave me a chill. He put one knee on his favorite stone chair and leaned out into the void, looking down the mountainside. "My guess is that if we hadn't made the turn here, we would have gone off the cliff doing at least thirty miles an hour."

He pulled a sleeve back and looked at his wristwatch. It was gold. I looked at my own watch. So far the trip had eaten up an hour. I'd had enough scenics for one day. I turned and walked away, but when I turned back to see if he was following, Trowbridge was on both hands and knees, still looking down.

"Mr. Trowbridge," I said, "I left the meter running."

He didn't respond. He kept leaning over the cliff.

I began walking toward him. "Mr. Trowbridge?"

I was walking sort of fast, reaching out with both hands. "Mr. Trowbridge!"

He backed off the rock and turned to look at me coming at him with both arms extended. I knew I must have looked strange, if not dangerous, but he didn't say anything. He began walking toward the cab.

The air was thin. I could barely breathe. I waited until he got into the backseat, then I shut the door for him. I walked around to the driver's side, my heart beating fast.

Mountains. Jaysus.

I started the engine, put the shift into gear, and waited for some cars coming up the road to pass by. Then Trowbridge said, "I've changed my mind about going to Buffalo Bill's grave."

I glanced back at him. "What's that?"

"I no longer wish to go to the top of the mountain. I went there so many times as a boy that I really don't need to see it again. I know exactly what it looks like. Or what it had looked like back then. It would break my heart to discover that the state parks department had modernized and improved the little museum and gift shop."

I nodded with understanding. The only change I like comes from the Denver mint.

"Where do you want to go now?" I said.

"Back to town," he said.

"Do you have a …" I began, then stopped. Then I went on. "… a place to stay?"

"Oh yes," he said. "New digs. It's located on north Broadway."

I pulled onto the road and pointed the hood downhill. It gave me the feeling that the spare tire in the trunk might roll onto my head. I hadn't driven down a road this steep since I was in San Francisco, except there aren't any roads in San Francisco that run five miles straight down. Maybe in the Mission District. I don't know.

When we got to the bottom and the road became perfectly level, I felt like I was leaning back in a rocking chair. I imagine that cowboys feel the same way when they take off their boots and put on tennis shoes. This might be one aspect of relativity overlooked by Einstein.

Trowbridge told me we could take I-70 back to Denver. I was relieved. Fast and furious—that's how I live, that's how I love, that's how I get rid of customers.

We took the 58th Avenue bypass out of Golden. After we connected with I-70 at Youngfield Street, Trowbridge leaned forward from the backseat and asked if I had a ballpoint pen that he might borrow.

My scalp prickled. I whipped a Bic from my breast pocket and handed it to him. "Keep it," I said. "I've got plenty extras," which was true. My plastic briefcase is a virtual treasure trove of extras: pens, pencils, Rolaids, coins, Kleenex, matchbooks, bandaids, pliers, crap, junk, garbage—everything a cab driver needs to keep the wheels of free enterprise greased and the tips rolling in. You never know what a fare might ask for. It's a learned thing. I once had a young man ask me if I had any condoms, but let's not get into that—save to say that, at the time, I didn't.

I reached up to adjust my rear-view mirror and saw Trowbridge hunched over one of his boxes that he was using as a kind of desk to steady his hand. He was writing slowly. Printing, I suspected. My mouth went dry. He was at it again, I felt certain. I felt like a jungle explorer watching a rare breed of animal do something no human being had ever see it do. You can let your imagination run riot on that one.

I debated whether or not to ask why he wrote things on money. I started mulling over ways to slip the question into a conversation.

When we got near the Platte Valley, I eased into the right lane so I could connect with the bustling morass of Interstate 25 that would take us toward downtown. I enjoy taking the off-ramp at the I-70/25 interchange. It's all overhead ramps and sweeping curves and multiple lanes that merge and expand and condense, making me feel like I'm sailing along the surface of a Mobius strip that finally straightens out and flings me south to Denver—I'm forced by the immutable laws of the stampede to really hot-rod it there for awhile.

But then the fun was over. I got off the highway and worked my way over to Broadway. We were at the outskirts of downtown. Both the AM radio and the Rocky radio were off, so there was a moment of silence, which I purposely chose to break. "What do you do for a living, Mr. Trowbridge?" I said. It was a gamble. I was being chummy. I figured he wouldn't mind since he had practically told me the story of his entire childhood on the way to Golden. I wanted to establish whether or not he was a counterfeiter.

"I am not currently employed," he said in a voice devoid of interest but also devoid of irritation, thank goodness. In my experience, unemployed people have a tendency to resent being found out. I don't know why, since they are the people I admire most in the world.

But he didn't elaborate. A lot of unemployed people do elaborate though, chattering like parakeets trying to justify their lack of a job—as if what a man did destined him as a person, fer the luvva Christ. I have found that what people do has no relevance at all as to who they are. I make judgments based solely on what television shows they watch, and I can't imagine anyone defining TV-watching as "doing" something.

CHAPTER 9

We were on Broadway getting close to midtown, so I finally glanced back and asked the big question: "What address are you going to?"

He surprised me by saying, "Anywhere along here will do."

I checked the landscape quickly, and did not see any apartment buildings. That area of north Broadway is a kind of ancient business district with a few gas stations and two-story, red brick office buildings and garages and cafés, but I didn't see any private digs. I glanced at the rear-view mirror and saw him tucking a billfold into his breast pocket. This was reassuring in its way. It indicated he had money. Whenever I ride in the backseat of a cab, which I occasionally do, I always make a big deal out of pulling my billfold from my back pocket and blatantly counting out my dough, because I know I look like someone who doesn't have any money.

There wasn't much traffic on the street, so I had no excuse to keep moving, but I was a bit concerned about the fact that he did not give me a specific address. I had figured we would be going to another tenement like the last two places that I had hauled him to. But as I had reminded myself scores of times during the past fourteen years—to no avail—it was none of my business. The ride was over. We had met briefly and now we were parting. Ships passing in the night. Hail and farewell. The lonesome life of a cabbie.

After I pulled over to the curb and parked, I quickly reached into my briefcase and scrounged a receipt, then turned and looked at Trowbridge, who was holding a number of bills toward me. The fare had come to $45.00.

"I need to give you a receipt," I said.

"That won't be necessary," he replied.

"What I mean to say is, I am required by PUC regulations to give you a receipt," I lied. "Any fare that comes to more than twenty dollars must be accompanied by a receipt for the taxi company's files." I was manufacturing this baloney at a hundred miles an hour, but I knew instinctively that I would get away with it because civilians don't know anything about cab driving. Not only was I not required to give him a receipt, I could have given him the ride free for all the city government cared. The only thing that interests them is my annual license renewal fee, the bastards.

"All right … whatever," Trowbridge said in a voice as disinterested as I knew it would be.

I plucked a fresh pen from my briefcase and bent down and carefully printed the following words on the Rocky Cab receipt: "You must not hold a job that you like."

I signed it, but I didn't jot down the cost of the fare.

I sat up straight and twisted around and took the money from him and gave him the receipt. He tucked it into his coat pocket without looking at it. So much for starting that conversation.

"That was a very pleasant trip," he said, as he shuffled his boxes together in a preamble to climbing out. "Thank you for putting up with my verbal effusion of rambling memories."

"You're welcome."

With that, Trowbridge climbed out of the taxi and shut the door. Hail and farewell. It was time to turn on the Rocky radio and get back into the game. The ride had taken almost an hour and a half, and had proven to be profitable. I figured that if I got a trip like that every hour and a half I could make lots of money per hour, but we've had that conversation.

I switched on the radio and began listening to the dispatcher yelling at the newbies. I pulled away from the curb and drove toward 18th Street. I turned right on 18th thinking about making my way to the Fairmont Hotel to see how long the line at the cabstand was, but instead I made another right and headed back toward Broadway.

I'm not very good at almost everything, but I'm especially not good at keeping vows. So instead of going to a hotel, I cruised up the street and stopped at the intersection and looked both ways along Broadway. Trowbridge was a block and a half away, and moving at a slow pace—a trudge. I sat at the corner awhile watching him until a car pulled up behind me and honked, then I pulled around the corner and proceeded to "tail" Trowbridge. I had done a bit of "tailing" in my time and had discovered that there's not much to it, thank goodness.

I pulled over and parked and watched him for a bit, and when he got far enough away I pulled back out and drove down the block, keeping my eye on his forlorn figure. Then I saw where he was going. It was a long, red brick building that covered half a block—the men's mission. It was a place where homeless men could go for a hot meal and a bed for the night.

I sat and watched as Trowbridge entered the front door with his two boxes, then I sat for a little while longer staring at a crowd of men hanging around the building: shabbily dressed, unshaven, unemployed men who had hit the rock-hard bottom of old Denver. I reached up to my shirt pocket and felt the money Trowbridge had given me. Why would he spend so much dough on a pointless cab trip? He could have used it to get himself a hotel room somewhere else. But then maybe it was his last dough and he wanted to spend it on something that was worthwhile to him because it wouldn't have lasted much longer anyway.

Jaysus.

I thought about going into the mission and giving the money back to him, but I knew he wouldn't accept it. When you've driven a cab as long as I have, you get to the point where you can read people, and his book read pride. I didn't know who he was or what his story was, but I knew he wouldn't have taken the money back. He hadn't wanted me to know where he was going, and it might have upset him to learn that I had followed him.

I thought about going into the mission and just dropping the dough into the donation box, assuming they had one, but then I thought, Give it up, Murph. You earned the dough fair and square, and Trowbridge would want you to keep it. Capitalism is capitalism. Leave the world-saving to the people who can afford guilt. You can barely afford Twinkies.

But that wasn't it. The real reason I didn't go to the mission and hand the money over was because I wanted to know if he had written a note on another fiver. In the end, uncontrollable curiosity kept me from doing the right thing. I believe Oppenheimer used the same excuse when he agreed to build the atom bomb.

But I felt so bad about all this that I didn't reach into my shirt pocket and pull out the dough and examine it. I felt like a voyeur, which is fairly normal, but for the first time in my life it held a taint of obscenity, which had never bothered me, but let's not get into that.

I felt melancholy as I drove away. During my drifter years I had floated around on the fringes among the down-and-out, but I had been young and was always able to find a job to afford a room. The handbills of Cleveland come to mind. I never really hit the skids. But even if I had hit the skids, I wouldn't have thought of it as "the skids." I would have thought of it as "romantic," like Jack Kerouac thumbing his way around the country and living in bowery rooms, when in fact he always had his mother to wire him money after he blew his stash on wine.

Writers.

Give me a break.

I drove to the Brown Palace and pulled in line behind four other cabs and settled in to read my paperback. But I couldn't concentrate. I still felt guilty. Not about the money but about the note I had written to Trowbridge on the spur of the moment. I would never have written that note if I'd known he was going to the men's mission. I had figured he was just moving to a new apartment somewhere along Broadway, and I wanted to get his reaction to my note. I was pretending to be a scientist, but I was just a jerk. A nosy jerk to boot. In other words, a social scientist.

After the cabs ahead of me pulled away with their fares and I was first in line, I forgot about Trowbridge and began reciting the universal cabbie mantra, "DIA, DIA"—universal in Denver anyway. I would imagine the cabbies out in Los Angeles mumble, "LAX, LAX," whenever they sit in front of the Beverly Hilton, assuming the Beverly Hilton has a taxi-stand. Never been there.

I got a Cherry Creek instead. It was a rich woman who wanted to go shopping at Saks Fifth Avenue. After she told me her destination, I drove in silence down Broadway, to Speer, to First Avenue. I didn't make chummy cab chatter. Rich women make me nervous. I've seen *Midnight Cowboy* five times.

After I dropped her off, I looked at the lousy seven dollars she had given me, then I placed the money in my plastic briefcase. I wanted to keep it separate from the Trowbridge dough. The Trowbridge dough was hanging heavy on my chest. I wanted to pull it out and shuffle through the bills, but at the same time I didn't want to. I felt like a kid who had figured out where his parents had hidden the Christmas presents and knew that he had it in his power to ruin his own surprise on Christmas morning, but couldn't bring himself to sneak a peek because it would be like saying goodbye forever to his childhood. That would be an unusually perceptive child, but that's how I felt. Okay. I'll admit it. I was eleven years old when I surreptitiously climbed into our attic in Wichita on Christmas Eve and said goodbye forever to my childhood. I just didn't know it at the time.

I pulled away from the front door of the mall and halted for the stoplight at the exit from the shopping center. The Rocky radio was on and I was only half listening to the dispatcher when the words "Cherry

Creek" resounded in my ears. I snatched the mike from the dash and said "One twenty-seven" before any other driver could grab it. This was the ideal situation. I was at the mall, and there was a fare at the mall. Lady Luck was with me. The address turned out to be a bank across the street. The dispatcher put the cap on my day by saying, "DIA."

I hung up the mike thinking about all the other cabbies grousing at my luck. A lot of cabbies lurk at the mall waiting for a big score, but a normal mall trip consists of a rich lady going home with her shopping bags, and that can get old. The Cherry Creek Shopping Center is not that far from the places where the rich folks reside, as I call 'em. A lot of old pros regularly work the mall because, I assume, they like being around rich folks. But each to his own, I always say.

I drove across the street and parked in a no parking zone where my fare would be able to see me when he came out the door of the bank. I wasn't worried about cops. Cops will give a cabbie a lot of slack as long as he remains inside his vehicle and doesn't stay too long in a zone. Sanctioned lawbreaking always makes me feel "special." I once made up a song called "Parking In A No-Parking Zone." I often make up songs as I drive my taxi, and sing them aloud to myself. Most of the songs have "colorful" lyrics, so I won't belabor the point, but I will say that cab driving, like living alone in a Yukon cabin, can lead to colorful thoughts.

While I was waiting for the fare to come out of the bank, I finally surrendered to my curiosity, as I knew I would. It was time to say goodbye forever to my childhood again.

I leafed through the money that Trowbridge had given me and found a fiver among the tens. I saw the following string of hand-printed words that went around the border of the bill like a neat row of tiny Christmas presents: "You must be compelled by an inner force to read books, listen to music, and view films which serve only to send you spiraling deeper into the bottomless pit of frustration."

CHAPTER 10

I was staring at Trowbridge's words when my fare came out of the bank carrying a briefcase. I quickly tucked the bills back into my shirt pocket feeling as if I had been caught reading a colorful lyric. The rear door opened and the man hopped in and said, "DIA," which served to ameliorate the sense of emotional shock I was experiencing. But maybe that was all for the best, i.e., get back up on that horse, pilgrim.

I tried to put the sentence out of my mind. I made idle chatter with my fare as we drove out to DIA. He told me he was an accountant. That didn't make me feel any better. But he did give me fifty bucks plus a tip at the terminal. I handed him a receipt with the cost of the ride purposely left blank. I decided I would make this my customary habit from now on, in honor of the Trowbridges of the world. But my fare pointed out the blank space to me, so I filled it in for him.

Accountants.

Give me a break.

I drove away from the airport after that. I had made one hundred dollars on two fares that day. I tried, and failed, to keep it from going to my head. I didn't feel so bad now, but I knew how meaningless it was. On my next shift I would be lucky to earn back my lease payment. As I say, everything evens out in the world of cab driving.

I took Peña Boulevard southwest—the only direction it goes, unless you include northeast—and when I merged with I-70 my cab, Rocky Mountain Taxicab #127, made a sudden lurching motion. It slowed, then sped up again. I glanced quickly at the gas gauge, which was reading three-quarters full. I cruised for another half mile, and it lurched a second time. I touched the gearshift to make sure I was properly in drive, then I tugged at the emergency brake handle just to make sure I hadn't forgotten to release it all the way at dawn.

I was doing the speed limit, all the dials on the dashboard seemed to be in working order, the engine sounded fine, yet the cab was making these strange bucking motions. It was acting the way vehicles do when they start running out of gas, which, if you are like me, you've had plenty of experience with. I couldn't figure it out, but I knew I had better get off the highway soon because something was wrong.

But then I thought, what the hell, I'm on I-70, I'll just keep going until I get to within the vicinity of the motor, then pull off the highway and take my cab in for a checkup by the Rocky mechanics. I was only ten minutes away from headquarters. I love the interstate highway system because no matter how far away you are from anything in terms of space, in terms of time you're right next to practically everything.

Then I noticed black smoke coming from the sides of the hood. Due to the fact that I had decided to drive to the motor rather than get off at the nearest exit, I now found myself traveling along a stretch of I-70 that did not have any exits. The Big Carruthers Deal was back, and smoke was beginning to seep into my cab through my heating vent.

I rolled my window down to create what my science teachers in high school called a "convection current." This was supposed to direct the smoke away from the heater, across my knees, and out the window, bypassing my face. It worked! I was stupefied. This was the first time that I could recall putting to use anything I had learned in high school. Latin and Algebra, of course, were useless.

Colorado Boulevard was coming up, so I stepped on the accelerator to move things along, but the engine didn't respond. The cab didn't speed up. It just kept moving at 55 m.p.h. So I began rhythmically tapping on the accelerator, expecting 127 to both speed up and slow down, but there was no detectable response. There seemed to be no connection at all between the gas pedal and the engine. The good news was that 127 didn't seem to be slowing down either. It was as if my cab was being pulled along by a UFO tractor-beam.

Colorado Boulevard came up, but because 127 seemed to be doing well I decided I would let the tractor-beam pull me past it and on to the exit at Vasquez Boulevard, a little farther along. To this day I don't understand why I did that. Instead of taking the Colorado exit, I made the same bad decision that I had made a few miles back, which was to stay on the highway. Why did I do that? In the midst of disaster I kept making plans. Was I in denial? Was I trying to salvage the Big Carruthers Deal? All I knew was that the "Exit Next Right" sign at Colorado whizzed past me in a blur, and I found myself still traveling along the highway with a useless gas pedal under my right foot and a smokescreen blowing across my knees.

My speed remained a constant 55. The Vasquez exit was coming up, so I tapped the brakes in preparation for getting off the highway, and guess what—I had no brakes.

Fortunately the highway there is sort of hilly. After Colorado you drop down a dip and rise again to the Vasquez exit, so I shifted into neutral and kept my foot away from the accelerator and felt 127 beginning to slow as I went up the rise toward the exit. I don't know what gravity is, and I'll bet Albert Einstein didn't either, but it worked that day.

By the time I swung onto the exit, I was going 25 m.p.h. The only problem was that I still didn't have any brakes. The exit ramp drops a good thirty feet from the highway down to Vasquez Boulevard at a steep angle. No problem though. I would just ease 127 over to the left side and let the tires rub against the curb. I had done this on slippery roads in the wintertime, so I was somewhat of an expert on desperation moves.

I took a fresh grip on the steering wheel and turned it to the left, and guess what—I had no steering.

Up until that moment the whole process of losing complete control over my vehicle had the quality of a metaphor. It mirrored my life, and I have never pretended to have any control over my life. As a consequence, I hadn't felt any particular panic until I found myself rolling down the exit ramp toward a highway filled with semi tractor-trailers. Vasquez Boulevard is an access road for truckers headed to the warehouse districts of north Denver, and there were plenty of trucks on the boulevard that day, baby.

At the bottom of the exit ramp was a stop sign, and I was headed right for it, and through it if I didn't do something fast. At this point I believe my Univac took control of my body, because suddenly I grabbed the steering wheel like a tackling dummy, threw my entire body weight against it, and 127 lurched to the left. The tires hit the curb and began slowing my vehicle. I came to a halt ten feet away from the stop sign.

Now that I was stopped, the smoke was no longer blowing across my knees. It was filling my cab. The engine was on fire. I grabbed my plastic briefcase, unbuckled my seatbelt, shoved the door open, and dove out. I landed on a strip of hard earth and rolled between the curb and a chain-link fence. It was just like in the movies, but it was real, and it hurt.

I got up and ran to the chain-link fence and turned and saw flames dripping from beneath the engine, probably caused by melting rubber and plastic parts. It created a little garden of fire beneath my engine. It was sort of pretty.

I leaned against the fence rubbing a bruised elbow and watching as the hood began to turn black. I knew then that 127 was a goner.

Pretty soon a cop car materialized and pulled into the exit ramp going the wrong way. It parked facing 127. The cop got out and asked if I was all right. I said yes. Then he drove slowly to the top of the ramp with his red light flashing to block traffic coming off I-70. Next came a fire truck with its siren wailing. Now that everything was a total loss, the government was showing up to take charge.

I watched with fascination as the paint job on 127 turned black, the fire progressing from front to back as if the taxi was in a car wash that spouted flames rather than water. First the paint job on the hood bubbled and turned black, then the roof, then the trunk. I saw the steering wheel become a ring of fire, then droop. By this time the firefighters had climbed off their truck in their yellow rubber spacesuits and started milling around. There were no fireplugs nearby, but I expected them to dash to the taxi with extinguishers and put out the flames. But no. They just wandered around letting my cab burn.

Then the right front tire exploded. A minute later the left front tire exploded. They sounded almost like hand grenades. I had once served in the army, and for some reason that I'll never understand, I was allowed to detonate a hand grenade, so I knew what they sounded like. The tire explosions weren't quite as impressive, but they still gave me a shock. I waited expectantly for the rear tires to explode, and I wasn't disappointed. Bang! Bang!

The firefighters began circling the hulk of 127 snuffing out rubber and plastic fires on the exit ramp. Apparently they had decided to just let it burn itself out. I didn't know why they weren't worried about the gas tank exploding. I wasn't worried either because I didn't think about it. This would explain why I drew close to the cab to peek into the interior to see the seats embroiled in an inferno of roiling flames. It was kind of cool. The whole scene was cool, until I realized I was out of a job.

I guess I was in shock. The sight of my taxi burning was sending an adrenaline stream though my nervous system that I simply was not used to. I felt giddy and gleeful. It reminded me of my first scotch. As the flames died down and the smoke dissipated and I saw the black hollow hulk of 127 resting tireless on the road, I began to come down from my natural high. The adrenaline rush was fading. I began to wonder how I was going to pay for having destroyed my taxi, because somehow, in some way, Rocky Cab would find out that I had not taken proper safety precautions, had not gotten off the highway before it caught fire, that I had pushed the envelope to the point of no return, that I had driven my taxi to death—although I didn't actually know how they would find this out because I sure as hell wasn't going to tell them.

I didn't have any idea how much taxicabs cost. I had never asked. And right then I didn't want to know. I began to grow afraid. I wanted my adrenaline back. I wanted to spend the rest of my life giddy. But it was no-go. The cop began walking toward me. It was just like in the movies. He was walking in slow motion. I was trapped. Caged. Nowhere to run.

"I called your company to let them know what happened," he said.

You fool! I wanted to scream, but I didn't. I just said, "Thank you."

"Are you sure you're okay?" he said.

It came to me fast. I should start coughing. I should buckle and fall to the ground, feign unconsciousness, put in a medical claim, sue the cab company, get a million dollars, and give 90 percent to a lawyer.

But who was I kidding? The lawyer for the insurance company would probably put me on a witness stand and tear me to ribbons. Fraud! Perjury! The Rock!

"I'm okay," I said.

The cop walked away in slow motion again. Maybe he was just tired.

The firefighters managed to pop the hood on 127, and after the smoke cleared they looked over the blackened ruins of the engine and wrote something down on a clipboard, but I was too leery to go see what they were writing. Then a firefighter strolled up to me and asked if I knew the taxi's PUC serial number, which was a long series of digits that had been stenciled on the left rear fender. I told him I didn't know it. I had been driving 127 for fourteen years and had never learned its PUC number—sort of like people who live in New York City and never visit the Statue of Liberty.

He shrugged and walked away. He didn't even ask for my name. I couldn't judge whether this was a good sign or a bad sign, or simply the sign of an inconsequential triviality. I abandoned a plan of trying to pass myself off as nothing more than an innocent bystander. That had been known to work in less pyrotechnic circumstances.

A tow truck arrived. The firefighters packed up and left. The cop drove off. Pretty soon it was just me and the tow driver. He went into his act. The black husk of 127 was dragged by chain onto the flatbed of his truck.

"Hop in," he said. "I'll give you a ride back to the cab company."

Rocky Cab was less than a mile away, and by then I was glad I hadn't driven all the way there only to let my supervisor, Hogan, and the cage man, Rollo, especially Rollo, watch my cab burn up. It would have been embarrassing and humiliating, the two words that best describe my life.

I climbed in and rode back to the motor staring out the front window and wondering what I was going to do for living now. I felt weak and fragile. It must have been an adrenaline hangover. I wasn't that familiar with adrenaline, since I never did anything that required it. I don't think I had walked faster than two miles an hour since I got out of the army.

Even though Rocky Cab was less than a mile away, it seemed to take forever to get there. The closer we got, the slower we seemed to go. This gave me time to parse my blunder. I thought about the fact that I had been cruising along Interstate 70 at a rate of 55 miles per hour with no brakes for perhaps seven miles. I had been traveling in a straight line most of the way. And it was only when I tried to make a hard left toward the curb that I discovered that the power steering was out. You may have experienced this yourself. Power steering has spoiled us Americans. I don't know how the pioneers made it to California without it.

Then I thought about what would have happened if there had been a traffic jam on I-70 and I had been forced to brake or pull some fast evasive action. I might have collided with the rear of another car. I had been sailing along oblivious to the danger I was in. I began to feel ill. I thought about asking the tow truck driver to pull over so I could open the door and vomit. But then I thought, *What if I can't vomit?* Think how embarrassing that would be. I would have to pretend to vomit, the ultimate humiliation. He would probably catch on.

By the time we got to Rocky Cab I was a mental wreck. The driver told me that he would take my cab to a junkyard to be turned into scrap, which was redundant, but I didn't say anything. My ego was too wounded to encourage him to speak more precisely. He let me out, then drove away. I stood in the silence of the street watching the black husk of poor ol' #127 disappearing down the road.

I took a deep breath and sighed. It was time to go into the main office and face the music, although I didn't actually know what "face the music" meant on a literal level. You would think that facing music would not be a bad thing, especially if it was Beatle music. Yet somehow the phrase "face the music" possessed a negative connotation that seemed appropriate. It was time to face the music. But there was one problem. I wasn't psychologically prepared to face the music.

CHAPTER 11

I stood in front of the door to the on-call room that would lead me up to the office where my supervisor Hogan would be waiting to speak to me about the cost of purchasing a new taxicab. I was still in shock of course, so I wasn't thinking very clearly. This might explain why I turned and walked away from the door, clutching my briefcase to my chest.

I went to the end of the block and turned at the corner and kept walking. I walked all the way to a bus stop. Even though there was a bench, I stood as I waited for the bus. I felt that if I sat down I might never be able to make myself stand up again. I kept hearing the tires explode. I kept seeing the paint job passing through the car wash from Hell, and I thought to myself, *Now I have become Murph, the destroyer of taxis.*

After awhile a bus came along and I got on and rode it all the way to Colfax Avenue. From there I transferred to a bus that would take me to within the vicinity of my crow's nest. It was only after I got on and made my way down the aisle that I began to come back to reality.

My Gawd! I was on a #15 bus!

Have you ever seen Fellini's *Satyricon*? Actually just about any Fellini film will do, but the sight of the passengers on the bus shook me out of my trance. I immediately tried to retreat back into the trance because I realized that I was now one of them.

My taxicab had just burned up, but rather than face the music I had run away. I had descended into the subterranean world of Denver's mobile underground. The faces of all the passengers looking at me would have become hideously distorted except that's how they normally looked.

But my knees did go weak. I found an empty seat and sat down hard. A young man was seated next to me, and I made the mistake of glancing at him.

"Hi," he said. "I'm an intellectual. Don't you think *The Graduate* is overrated?"

I frowned at him. "Do you mean the movie?" I said.

"Yes, don't you think it's overrated?"

I shrugged. "As a light romantic comedy, I think it's okay."

I was lying of course. I love that movie. I'm a Baby Boomer. But I was talking to an intellectual, and he had me scared.

"I much prefer *Carnal Knowledge*," he said.

I began to feel dizzy. Was I discussing the seminal works of Mike Nichols with a film buff or with a master of the double entendre? I reached for the buzzer and yanked it. The bus buzzer I mean.

I got off near the capitol building. The sun was flashing off the golden dome. It made me think of money. It made me think of the cost of a brand new taxi. There was only one place to go: Sweeney's Tavern. I wasn't sure what I needed right then—a good talking to, a new life, a horsewhipping, take your pick—but whatever I needed, I knew I wouldn't find it at Sweeney's, thank God.

I walked down The Hill and across Broadway. I wended my way toward the fringes of the financial district where Sweeney's is located. But then I realized that my route would take me past the Brown Palace Hotel. It would take me past the taxi stand. It might even take me past … Big Al.

It was then that I fully realized what I had done. I had left the scene of an accident! My God, what was I doing in the middle of downtown Denver when I was supposed to be reporting to my supervisor at Rocky Cab? I suddenly felt like I was living in some sort of twisted dream—not quite a nightmare, not yet anyway. I began to wonder if I had inhaled too much smoke. I did feel lightheaded. Was it the adrenaline? Was it the sight of my longtime taxi friend turning to ash? Was it the fact that I had to find another job? I decided to go with door number three. What would I do for a living now? There was no way that I was ever going to be allowed to drive a cab again.

I devised a circuitous route around the Brown Palace and continued on my way toward Sweeney's, wondering how I was going to earn money now that the best of all possible jobs had been taken away from me through my recklessness and ineptitude. Most of the jobs I had lost in my lifetime were due merely to ineptitude—although one time I was suspended from Rocky Cab while being investigated for murdering an eighteen-year-old girl, but that's a long story. Let's drop it.

As I worked my way across town I began to wonder about my future. I don't know why, since apparently I didn't have one. I was a man on the run. God only knew, but the police had probably been informed that I was missing. I felt like a draft dodger. The Feds would be waiting for me if I ever made the foolish mistake of returning to my crow's nest. I would be forced to flee to Canada, wear bell-bottoms, and smoke pot. These were the thoughts that tormented me as I wended my way toward Sweeney's Tavern, clutching my plastic briefcase to my chest.

Sweeney wasn't on duty. The place was empty of customers right then. The pre-lunch crowd would be served by Harold, a recent graduate of a bartending school. I had once toyed with the idea of going to bartending school, but I gave it a thumbs-down when I realized I would be spending all my time serving drinks to people like me.

"Top o' the morning to ye, Murph me boy!" Harold said.

It's not that I dislike Harold, I simply dislike his cheap imitation of Sweeney. Harold is twenty-two years old, and Sweeney is in his fifties. Harold is from the Denver suburb of Thornton, and Sweeney is from the Ol' Sod—Chicago.

Harold is also a runner, which he will be glad to elaborate upon if he ever sees you coming. He runs laps on the indoor track at the YMCA every day. Why, I don't know. When I first made the mistake of letting him know my name, he began telling me that I ought to accompany him to the "Y" for a run. "I really think you would enjoy running," he said, in the same strangely enthusiastic monotone that people utilize when promoting Transcendental Meditation.

One evening I finally had it out with him. I looked him in the eye and said, "Don't ever mention running to me again, Harold." I even went so far as to use my "scary" voice.

"Why not?" he said.

"When I was in the army, my drill sergeants told us that back in the brown-boot army they were forced to run ten miles every morning. After I heard that horrifying story, I bled from the ears for a week."

The letter "Y" never came from Harold's mouth again. "Morning," I said lethargically. I don't know why I bothered.

Harold has never grasped the nuances of symbolism, allegory, or snub.

"Starting a wee bit early today, are we not?" Harold said as he filled a glass with draft.

"Actually no," I said, as I handed him a sawbuck and picked up my beer. "It's late for me. I just dropped a woman off at her apartment. We had a date that lasted three days."

Harold's youth betrayed him. His eyes almost popped out of his head. His cheeks turned pink. He nervously placed the ten-spot in the cash drawer, pulled out my change, and gave it to me with a trembling hand. It took all my willpower to refrain from asking if he was a Catholic.

I carried my beer over to a corner of the tavern. It was fairly dark in the room. Sweeney keeps the electric bulbs off in the daytime, so the light comes in through the picture windows, which are subtly tinted. The floor of Sweeney's is naked wood, and most of the booths are unpadded, although there are a few padded booths for the ladies. I've never actually seen any ladies in Sweeney's, but let's not get into that.

I hid myself in a corner booth adjacent to an upright piano. There is no jukebox in Sweeney's. Anybody who wants to hear music has to BYO.

This includes singing, as well as playing musical instruments that often make their way into the bar—street musicians show up every now and then with guitars or fiddles or flutes.

Just for your info, Sweeney does not include "tambourine" in his lexicon of musical instruments.

It was not yet noon, and there I was sipping a beer. I was glad Sweeney wasn't on duty. He doesn't make it into the tavern until Happy Hour. Harold doesn't have enough years under his belt to ride herd on the Happy Hour crowd. If I had entered Sweeney's before noon on a Monday and Sweeney himself had been there, he might not have served me a beer. He might have been too busy calling my Maw in Wichita.

I set my briefcase in front of me on the tabletop, but then shoved it aside. I felt as if I was shoving aside the past fourteen years of my life. I started thinking about 127 and all the things we had been through together, all the fares I had driven around Denver, all the people whose personal lives I had gotten involved in, to my regret. I thought about the scorched body of 127 being carted away on the rear of the tow truck. I began to feel a bit blue.

"Pretzels?"

Harold was standing by my table holding a wicker basket. "Just set them there," I said, pointing at the tabletop.

"Who do you think's going to win the pennant this year?" he said.

I almost collapsed with boredom. Harold was trying so hard to be a bartender that it was painful to watch. Baseball season hadn't even started yet.

"The Black Sox," I said.

He stuck out his lower lip and nodded wisely.

"Could I have a napkin?" I said, before he could talk again.

He hurried away. I prayed to God that a customer would come into the tavern to distract him ... and I'm not much of a praying man. But my prayer was answered. Two ladies came through the doorway and sat down on barstools. I assumed they were ladies, but I wasn't interested in finding out. Not before noon, brother.

I took a few swallows of beer and tried to remember what I had been doing before Harold had set the pretzels in front of me. Ah yes, the death of 127 … or perhaps I should say the manslaughter! I assumed they were looking for me by now. The police were probably interrogating the tow truck driver. Hogan would be frantic and enraged. The execs at the insurance company would be hounding him to track me down. My life was an absolute mess. I took another sip of beer.

"What can I do for you ladies?" They began giggling.

I looked toward the bar. Harold had made the classic bartender blunder of saying "do" when he meant "get." I pitied Harold. Those "ladies" were going to make mincemeat out of him before their bender came to an end, probably in the rear of a police van. And for all I knew, I would end up joining them on the ride downtown. The charge? Leaving the scene of an accident!!!

Then it occurred to me that I had not actually left the scene of an accident. The policeman had made his investigation and then had driven off. The incident was over by the time I had climbed into the tow truck. I frowned. What had I been thinking? The shock of seeing my taxi burn up, plus the adrenaline rush, must have clouded my mind. All I had done was flee in order to avoid being handed a bill for thousands of dollars. Hell, I've done that plenty of times.

I started thinking it over. Nobody knew where I was. Maybe Hogan was still waiting for me to show up. What would make him think I had fled anyway? Right at this moment he might be thinking I was holed up in the can or something. In fact, he might not be thinking about me at all.

But doesn't everybody spend all their time thinking about you? my ego murmured.

I decided to order a shot of scotch. I pulled out the beer change that I had stuffed into my shirt pocket. Old habits die hard. But I was no longer a cab driver, so I also pulled out my billfold. I would use that from now on instead of my shirt pocket. I told myself that I might as well get used to living like everybody else on earth. It wouldn't take long to achieve that goal, since I was unemployed and watched TV ninety hours a week.

I sorted through the bills—a fiver and some ones. The fiver was face down, so I turned it over out of money-handler habit—and my hair almost stood on end. Printed in tiny letters above Abraham Lincoln's head were the words: "You must be prepared at any given moment to relinquish all semblance of dignity."

CHAPTER 12

"Where did this come from?" I demanded. I was standing at the bar.

Harold looked at me with naked fear in his eyes. I was wedged between the two ladies. There was no one else in the bar.

"Oh," he said. "Your napkin. I forgot."

He plucked a paper napkin off a stack near a beer spigot. I grabbed the napkin and tossed it to the floor. "This five-dollar bill, where did it come from?"

"The cash register," he said.

The women leaned away from me in opposite directions.

I held the bill up for Harold to see. "This! Where did you get this?"

He raised his right hand and pointed at the cash register. I realized that I had actually found a way to shut Harold up, the last thing on earth I wanted right then.

"Are we in your way?" one of the women said.

I lowered the bill and edged out from between the women. I moved around to one side and held the fiver up again.

"Harold, this five-dollar bill, did a customer give it to you?"

He nodded. "Customers are the only people who give me money."

I knew the feeling. "What I meant to say was, did you get this fiver from a customer today?"

He looked down at it. "I must have. Customers are the only …"

"What did he look like?"

"Who?"

"The man who gave you this five-dollar bill! Did he look like Bozo the Clown?"

The women started giggling.

"I'm sorry, Murph," Harold said nervously. "If you want, I can call Sweeney."

"Call Sweeney, doll-face," one of the women said.

"Yeah, call Sweeney," the other said. "Get him out of bed." The word "Sweeney" worked its magic on me. I calmed down.

If I had been drunk, it would have scared me.

I raised my empty hand palm-outward, and shook my head no. "I'm sorry, Harold. I didn't mean to make you call Sweeney. In fact, it would be best if you didn't mention to Sweeney that I was in here this morning. It's just that I gave this five-dollar bill to a customer last night and here it is again," I lied. "I recognize it. See this handwriting? It's the same bill that I gave to a fare, and I was so surprised to see it again that I thought I was having one of those experiences you read about in *Ripley's Believe It or Not*. The fare was a guy older than me. Bristly hair. Unshaven. He wore a mismatched coat and pants. Actually he looked more like Emmett Kelly than Bozo. I was just wondering if he was in here this morning."

Harold nodded.

"What?" I said. "What's that nod? What do you mean?"

"I know the guy," Harold said. "He did come in here this morning."

"Trowbridge!" I said. I meant to say "Trowbridge?" with a question mark, only it came out with an exclamation point. I was losing control.

"I don't know his name," Harold said. "He comes in here every once in awhile. He came in about nine. He was waiting outside for me to open the door. I think he's a drunkard."

"Call Trowbridge," a woman said.

I looked at the words on the bill. "Does he always write things on money?"

Harold shrugged. "I don't know."

God I hated Harold. What kind of bartender doesn't know who gives him what? But then I remembered that Harold was a recent graduate of bartending school. He hadn't been around long enough to acquire the financial acumen second nature to bartenders, cab drivers, and IRS agents. We know exactly who gives us what, especially IRS agents.

Nevertheless, he had answered my question. He had also answered a question I hadn't even asked, one that had been haunting me ever since the first ride I had given to Trowbridge. Was Trowbridge passing judgment on me? No. Apparently he was doing it to everybody.

I smiled at Harold. "Crazy, huh? I give a guy a five-dollar bill, and the next day I get it back. It makes you wonder if capitalism isn't just a shell game."

Harold grinned, but it was sickly. He had seen me drunk before, but he had never seen me bemused. "I'll tell you what," I said. "This Ripley deal calls for a celebration. I hardly ever have strange things happen to me, so why don't I buy a drink for everybody in the bar?"

Fortunately there were only two ladies in the bar. They each asked for a shot of Johnnie Walker Red. The bill came to five dollars. Crazy, huh?

I pulled a different fiver from my billfold, imitating a normal person. I examined it before handing it over. Abe was mum.

"I gotta be taking off," I said.

"Stick around, kiddo," one of the women said.

"I would," I said, "but I think I'm still on duty."

"What are you, a cop?"

"Worse—I'm a cab driver."

"I didn't know cab drivers are allowed to drink beer on duty," she said.

"Call Ripley," her friend said.

"I'm not actually driving," I said. "My taxicab burned up this morning."

"Burned up!?" Harold said with two punctuation marks.

Sometimes I don't know which I hate worse, Harold or my mouth. I resigned myself to the fact that Sweeney would get the lowdown by the end of Happy Hour. Sweeney was a lot like my Maw, except me ol' Mither gave up bartending a few years after she got married.

I left the tavern. I had an agonizing decision to make. The only way I could get back to the motor was to take a #15 bus, or else go to a hotel and take a Rocky Cab. Hobson's Choice: death or humiliation. I chose death. I walked over to Colfax and climbed onto the first 15 that rolled up to the curb.

So there I was, standing in front of the door to the on-call room at Rocky Cab, just as I had been standing there almost two hours earlier. I felt like Dennis Weaver in that episode of *The Twilight Zone* where he kept waking up in jail after being executed over and over again. I wondered if that was his first dramatic role after *Gunsmoke*. I once saw Dennis Weaver being interviewed on TV—he was building a house out of recycled tires. Crazy, huh?

I shoved the door open and walked inside. I was now prepared to face the music. A few cabbies were milling about the room. Nobody paid any attention to me. I walked up to the cage where Rollo was eating a donut. He stopped in mid-chew and stared at me. "Murph!" he said.

"I've come back," I said humbly.

I braced myself to endure an avalanche of malicious condescension— I had earned it, and Rollo was a pro.

"We heard your cab burned up," he said. "You've still got four hours left on your lease. Do you want another taxi?"

"What?" I said.

"Four-oh-nine is available," he said.

"What?"

"Chuck Ferguson is off sick today. You can use his cab."

"What?"

"He asked us to assign it to anyone who wants to use it."

"What?"

"Do you feel all right, Murph?"

"What?"

It went on like this for a while longer. I won't bore you with any more whats. Rollo handed me a trip-sheet and the key to 409, Chuck Ferguson's hack. Chuck is an old pro. He's been driving almost twenty years. He owns the cab.

I had never seen Rollo like this before though. His attitude was all wrong. He should have been heaping malicious condescension on my head and taking enormous pleasure in my misfortune, but he seemed merely fascinated by it. But maybe that's the same thing.

"Does Hogan know my cab burned up?" I said.

"Yeah," Rollo said.

That's all he said. It was as if the burning of a taxicab meant nothing to these people.

I walked out of the on-call room in a daze. I wandered through the dirt lot where all the taxis were parked, found 409, and climbed in. I sat behind the steering wheel staring at the Rocky Mountains in the distance. It was like that scene in *The Catcher in the Rye* when Holden Caulfield said that every time he crossed a road he felt like he was disappearing. I felt like I had just crossed a road.

It was only then that the impact of losing my old friend of fourteen years finally hit me. I would never see poor ol' #127 again. I would like to say that I wept, but I kept thinking about those exploding tires. Bang! Bang! Bang! Bang! It sort of made me laugh.

I started 409 and headed out. I had rarely driven any other taxi than 127. It happened occasionally, as when my hack was in for repairs, but I almost always got assigned another company cab. No frills, in other words. But a driver-owned taxi is a study in frills. Witness the Christmas-tree odor-eater dangling from 409's rear-view mirror. And that's just for starters. The front and back seats weren't upholstered in your standard fake Naugahyde plastic covers that got damn cold in the wintertime—409 had corduroy. The steering wheel had an elastic terry-cloth cover, and the floor mats weren't made in Detroit—my guess was mail-order. And of course the headliner wasn't your standard vinyl, it was a soft fabric, lemon-lime tinted in keeping with the Christmas motif. I kept reaching up and touching it. And the AM radio? AM hell, Ferguson had AM/FM, plus tape deck, plus stereo speakers installed in the rear window. I felt like I was driving a bachelor pad. But enough of descriptive prose. You probably had your fill of that in high school. I know I did. The point is that a driver-owned taxi is classier in every way than a company car—cleaner, fancier, cushier, and more pleasant smelling. Ferguson's privately owned taxicab served to remind me of what a pile of junk I had been driving around for the past fourteen years. I began to resent it.

But then I told myself that form is less important than content, whether you're talking English literature or urban transportation. The purpose of a taxicab is people moving, pure and simple. Who needs all these bells and whistles? They're not going to increase the number of trips you get from hotels. They're not going to add to the number of calls that come over the radio. Professionalism, that's what puts money into a cabbie's pocket. The difference between 127 and 409 was the difference between a dragster and a French poodle! By God, if Daniel Boone was a cabbie he would have driven 127!

Yeah, that's what I told myself. But who was I kidding? I would rather read William Faulkner than Mickey Spillane. I loved 409 with all its frills and knickknacks and dangly things. I started thinking wild thoughts about buying a cab of my own and fixing it up like Caesar's palace. The Vegas Caesar, not the Rome one. But again, who was I kidding? Why would I buy a taxi? Hacking wasn't my life. My life was writing novels. But maybe they're the same thing.

I headed downtown. Ferguson's Folly had a full tank of gas. This made me feel rich, even though I would have to top it off before I turned it in. As Milton Friedman insists, there is no such thing as a free anything. As I drove, I kept my itchy fingers away from the AM/FM radio. I tuned in the Rocky dispatcher and began listening for bells. In the days to come I was going to work the downtown beat exclusively with the microphone clutched in my right hand, waiting, always waiting, for one bell in particular. For one familiar address. For one familiar name: *Trowbridge*.

He would be waiting outside.

CHAPTER 13

I started hanging out at Sweeney's after work.

I went there at the end of the same day I received the fourth fiver from Trowbridge, although I no longer believed he was directing his cosmic messages at me, if cosmic they were. They sure sounded cosmic. When I was in college I attended an introductory seminar for Transcendental Meditation, so I knew a thing or two about cosmic consciousness. Well, maybe one thing. The Maharishi's teachings said that if you meditated twice a day for ten years you would attain cosmic consciousness, although he didn't say exactly what that was. But I decided against signing up for the training class. Ten years was too long to wait. Ironically, if I had taken the training I would have become cosmic twelve years ago. Bummer.

I was worried about Sweeney though, as I walked through the swinging doors that night. I didn't trust Harold. He might have squealed. But I had to go to Sweeney's because I wanted to run into Trowbridge "outside the cab," as we hacks refer to the real world. I wanted to see if Trowbridge wrote sentences on money while he sat in bars. If he was "a drunkard" as Harold had said, I wanted to observe him in his natural habitat. I wanted to observe a man who woke up each day in a state of total despair without looking at my bathroom mirror.

The joint was crowded when I walked in. It wasn't jumping though. Sweeney doesn't allow that. He's a big guy, Sweeney. Anybody who starts "jumping" in his bar had better be doing the River Dance.

Sweeney was busy tending bar when I slipped in, so he didn't notice me. I wanted to keep it that way. I planted myself in a corner and watched the door in case Trowbridge entered with a pocket full of fivers and a fresh Bic aching to pass judgment on the world. Pretty soon Kelley came over to my table. Kelley was a waitress.

"What can I get for you, Murph?" she said with a saucy smile. She's been around. She knows the difference between "get" and "do," unfortunately.

"A draught," I said.

I once passed through Seattle during my drifter years, and learned that people there say "schooner" when they order a mug of beer. I discovered it when I walked into a waterfront bar and asked for a "draught" and the bartender looked at me as if I had ordered a cow. As soon as I finished my schooner I got out of Seattle. While I was waiting at the bus depot I asked a man pushing a broom if he had been in town when they had filmed the Elvis Presley movie, *It Happened at the World's Fair*. He gave me a disgusted look and walked away. I liked that.

I had been in Sweeney's about an hour when Sweeney finally noticed me sitting alone at the table. I knew he would spot me sooner or later. I read his face fast. I didn't see any disgust. Word of advice: don't ever mention Elvis to Sweeney. 'Nuff said. But apparently Harold hadn't squealed about me showing up for a beer before noon on Monday. Sweeney just gave me a nod from behind the bar but didn't make a beeline for the phone. My Maw is on his speed-dial. So Harold had come through for me after all. Maybe he really would make a good bartender someday. Or maybe he had just forgotten. Or maybe—just maybe—I wasn't on Harold's list of top priorities. Take your pick.

Trowbridge didn't show up that night. Nor the next night, nor the next. I began to get the feeling he was a day drinker. Anybody my age who stands outside a bar at nine in the morning probably fulfills his commitments by Happy Hour. I decided to change my tactic and start dropping in at Sweeney's in the morning, even though this would entail having "conversations" with Harold.

The first morning that I showed up I ordered a cup of steaming joe and told Harold I was taking my nine o'clock taxi break, which of course wasn't true—taxi driving itself is just one long endless break on the road to the boneyard. But he stuck his lower lip out and nodded wisely, then asked me how come they don't have goalies in basketball like they do in hockey. It took all my willpower to show up the next morning, but I had to do it. I wanted to see Trowbridge in action.

The next morning Harold asked me if it was possible to make cheese out of a dog's milk. I said yes. Then he asked if ants could hold their breath.

I finally gave up hope. I realized I was making an error that I had made many times in my life, which was pretending that I had any control over anything. Whether my luck was good or bad, I myself was not in the loop. Fate was my designated driver. For example, one night during my drifter years I was passing through Des Moines and happened on a school fair taking place in a parking lot adjacent to a Catholic church. I stopped to look at the strung lights and balloons, the kids and the cakewalks. It reminded me of Wichita. I had attended Blessed Virgin Catholic Grade School in Wichita, and they held a fair every spring. They set up booths where you could toss darts at balloons or softballs at metal milk bottles. Games like that. For one thin dime you could take a ride with Lady Luck, although that was a venial sin, but Monsignor O'Leary always gave the congregation absolution for the evening.

The Des Moines bash started to make me feel a bit homesick. But since I am averse to all forms of sentimentality that aren't broadcast on television, I started to walk away. And then I saw it. A Bingo game. There were scores of people sitting at long tables that looked like they had been hauled out of a cafeteria. I'm third generation Irish-Catholic so I caved in and bought a card. It was only a quarter. I sat down at a long table across from an elderly couple who were working eight cards simultaneously. The man at the microphone started calling out letters and numbers, and five minutes later I found myself hollering "Bingo!" I had won. My take was eighteen dollars. Just enough for a bus ticket out of Des Moines.

But when I yelled "Bingo!" the couple across from me threw down their markers with disgust, got up, and stormed away. They obviously had been sitting there for hours trying to win. It seemed like every place I went I disgusted people. But I learned something significant that night. I learned that life is unfair to everybody except me. I liked that. It's been my guiding light ever since.

On the night that I got home from Sweeney's after giving up hope of seeing Trowbridge, I cooked my usual hamburger, ate it, and did the dish. I carried my beer into the living room and removed my copy of *The Stranger* from the bookshelf and opened it to the fifteen dollars that had come from the Trowbridge taxi fares. I took the money out and put the book back on the shelf, then I sat down in my easy chair and laid all the bills out in the order that I had received them, including the Harold fiver.

Each bill had an observation, or a direct order, or a saying, or I don't know what, written on it. I read them concurrently, as if they were sentences in a paragraph:

"You must wake up each day in a state of total despair. You must harbor a secret in your past so dreadful and shameful that the mere thought of it sends you lurching violently to the nearest liquor store. You must be compelled by an inner force to read books, listen to music, and view films which serve only to send you spiraling deeper into the bottomless pit of frustration. You must be prepared at any given moment to relinquish all semblance of dignity."

I pondered these words for a few moments, then I pulled out my billfold, removed a fiver, and in imitation of Trowbridge's handwriting I wrote a caption of my own, the same one I had written on the receipt: "You must not hold a job that you like."

I placed the five alongside the others to see whether it stacked up in both form and content. The printing itself looked good—Trowbridge himself might have written it. But I was unsure of the content. It seemed a bit thin in comparison with his own phraseology, yet I felt it captured the spirit of his mind-set. But what exactly was his mind-set? Why did he write things down on money? I realized that in spite of my jungle-explorer analogy, I hadn't really learned anything new about the man the last time I had seen him. I hadn't confronted him about his strange messages. I had merely jotted down a one-liner on a receipt as if I was playing a game and waiting for his reaction. But only now did I realize that by doing such a thing, I may have crossed the line!

At some point he might have read what I had written and decided that for some reason I was mocking him. I've had similar experiences in my life, usually when I was trying to be witty around strangers. I don't mean cab fares, where you can usually get away with lame jokes, but at parties or bars where I've had too much to drink. This was often in bumbling conjunction with my eagerness to get to know a woman, but let's move on.

I stowed the money back in *The Stranger,* including my own by-line. I decided to view the twenty-five dollars as a kind of surplus that I would save for the day when I was flat busted, which arrives every now and then. I doubted I would see Trowbridge again, doubted I would ever get a satisfactory solution to the mystery of the talking money.

I put the book away and shut it all out of my mind by turning on the TV and channel-surfing until I hit an episode of *Gilligan's Island,* the most effective means I know to remove all rational thought from my mind. It also does a job on irrational thought, so by the time I kicked off my Keds and collapsed into bed, I had forgotten all about Trowbridge. Instead, I started thinking about the fact that I would have to drive again the next day because I was already twenty bucks down for the week, thanks to Trowbridge. So there he was, back in my thoughts. Crazy, huh?

The next day I hauled myself out of bed thinking that I needed to earn seventy-five bucks just to make up for my losses. I began to castigate myself. I told myself that this was my punishment for getting involved, even peripherally, in the life of a fare. I might end up having to work a full week when the rent wasn't even due. This made me mad at myself. I don't mind if other people get mad at me because I'm used to it, but I hate it when I get mad at myself because it's impossible to turn on my heel and walk away in a huff and refuse to speak to me again. I've tried it plenty of times, believe me.

As I guided my heap to Rocky Cab, I kept a grim look on my face. This was to remind me that I had to earn an extra twenty-five bucks— half a day's pay!—because I had forsaken the vow that I made to myself at least once a month, sometimes once a week, depending on the psychological makeup of my backseat. I told myself that I ought to recite my vow once a day, like saying the Pledge of Allegiance each morning in grade school, i.e., renew the pledge every twenty-four hours or suffer the moral and political consequences.

CHAPTER 14

After I arrived at work I was assigned Rocky Mountain Taxicab #123, a relic from the early days when Rocky Cab had wangled the right to open for business on the mean streets of Denver. I wasn't around then, and the stories I heard from the old pros made me glad I wasn't. The other cab companies in town opposed allowing another franchise to cut into their profits. I won't name the companies that opposed it, but that should be fairly easy for you to deduce since there were only three at the time.

But drivers for the other companies insisted that there weren't enough shoes on the street to accommodate a fourth company, that all the drivers would suffer loss of income if another franchise was approved, that business would suffer, that passenger safety would be at risk, and on and on and on. But I could tell that it all came down to one thing: money.

What everybody really wanted was to be the only cab company in town, or better yet, the only driver. I would be rolling in dough if I drove the only hack in Denver. I could make ten runs to DIA every day and still have time to quit early. I'd be giving service with two smiles.

Anyway, #123 was a relic—a word obviously derived from the Latin noun for "wreck." The paint job was faded and rusted here and there, and the interior of the cab was stripped to the bare bones, meaning it didn't have an AM radio. If I wanted to rock on the job I would have to pick up a transistor from K-Mart, but that would have set me back at least three bucks. Tough call. I've always claimed to be a big fan of both silence as well as rock 'n' roll, and I hate it when my bluff is called. But I figured if my fares could stand twelve hours of my humming, so could I.

I really started missing poor ol' #127 then. I hadn't approached Hogan to ask if an arrangement was going to be made to find me another permanent—if that's not an oxymoron—taxi. In the end, though, I was permanently assigned Rocky Mountain Taxicab #123, the last of the hundred-numeral vehicles that had been bought at an auto auction long before I became a cabbie. Nobody else wanted it. Or to put it another way, everybody else refused it.

But this was how I had always lived my life. I accepted whatever life dished out and hoarded it. I had been assigned #127 fourteen years earlier simply because it was available, and when newer, better cars came into the possession of the company, I told Hogan I was happy with 127, which was true. I knew 127 inside and out, and understood its quirks and foibles, whatever foibles are. I guess I'm sort of like a writer who is afraid of personal computers and prefers to stick with his ancient Smith Corona rather than going through the intimidating, excruciating, humiliating experience of learning how to press Control-S.

Oh yeah. I've seen Control-S before. I go to the office supply store whenever my typewriter runs low on ribbons, and I sometimes walk down the computer aisle pretending to be slightly lost, when in fact I am secretly looking at the latest models of PCs that I'm afraid of buying. It's not the expense—well, it's partly the expense—well, it's mostly the expense—but it's also the idea of learning something new that keeps me from walking up to a computer and touching that terrifying mouse thing. Okay. I'll admit it. I'm afraid that if I press Control-S, the monitor will explode in my face.

But I figure my parents sent me through twelve years of Catholic schooling and I survived without a computer in the classroom, so obviously the human race doesn't need machines that can perform millions of complex mathematical computations in one second. If I don't need something, then nobody else needs it—that's my philosophy.

A lot of cabbies I'm acquainted with are also unpublished novelists, and some of them do own PCs, and they tell me I ought to buy one because I could do my rewrites in a single weekend rather than taking six months to retype a manuscript. But I just laugh in their faces. I never do rewrites. I'm from the Jack Kerouac school of rejection slips. One draft, and bang, into the mailbox she goes. So right there I've saved thousands of dollars by not buying a PC. I tell ya, Madison Avenue oughta be hung.

After gassing up and buying my morning's "supplies" at a 7-11, I drove directly to the Brown Palace and got in line at the cabstand. Since I had no AM radio I had to satisfy myself with reading a paperback in silence and chewing my supplies. It had been days since I had driven a "normal" shift and I wanted things to get back to the way we were. I always end up doing this after getting involved one way or another in the personal lives of my fares. Reading, eating, and offering inane chatter to my customers, that's a normal shift for me. That's how things had been going for the past few months, until I encountered Trowbridge. I had come close to getting deeply involved with Trowbridge, but I had managed to skirt the quagmire. I figured it wasn't a sign so much as a nudge from the gods to remind me to squelch anything that had even the faintest taint of ambition. Doing things on purpose never pays, it only exacts.

I ended up with a passenger out of the Brown who wanted to go to a car dealership on south Broadway near Arapahoe Road, which was a decent fare, almost as good as the Tech Center. It was a businessman in the market for a Cadillac. I was curious to know why anyone staying at a hotel would buy a Cadillac, but one of the gods told me to stay out of it—I think it was Thor. I earned twenty-five bucks right out of the chute, so I was feeling pretty good.

Afterwards I pulled into a McDonald's parking lot to fill out my trip-sheet. I rarely do this right after dropping off a fare because I'm too busy eating a Twinkie or else racing back to a hotel to get ahead of all the other cabbies racing back to the same hotel. But on the occasion that I do fill out the sheet right away I feel competent, and tell myself I ought to do this every time so that I will never get behind in my paperwork. I feel like I'm my own Maw telling me to do my homework on Friday night right after school. "Then ye'll have the whole weekend free to play," she used to say. Ha! What do mothers know of Fridays? Fridays are for unwinding with a stack of comic books, and Saturdays are for playing. Sunday night, that's the time to do your homework—right after Ed Sullivan and five minutes before you collapse into bed. Any kid who can't do his homework in five minutes deserves an F anyway. Ergo, I rarely fill out my trip-sheets as soon as a fare leaves the backseat.

I was in south Denver, so I decided to listen to the dispatcher as I drove toward midtown. That's the way a cabbie puts money into his pocket: position yourself like Fast Eddie Felson running a rack of pool balls, sinking shots left and right, and working your way back to Ames without getting your thumbs broke.

Then I got an L-2.

"One twenty-three, one twenty-three, el-two," the dispatcher said.

It seems like you're always a million miles away from the motor when you get an L-2. "L-2" is a secret code that means, "return to the motor." Old pros never argue with an L-2. The only drivers who argue with an L-2 are newbies. It's always fun to listen to the dispatcher yelling at a newbie who complains that he's out at DIA or way down south at the Tech Center when he gets an L-2. An L-2 is a fairly serious call because it usually means Hogan wants to talk to you about something important, and "important" can mean virtually anything. But Hogan is a good supervisor, and he would never call a cabbie in to the motor unless it was a serious situation.

I plucked the mike from the dashboard. "Check." I replaced it and resigned myself to driving all the way up Broadway and making my way over to Rocky Cab near the I-70 viaduct. I checked the odometer as I drove. It came to one million miles. There went my Cadillac profits.

I had been L-2'd quite a few times in my career, but I don't want to get into them because they are all long stories with disastrous endings. I wasn't worried though. I thought it might have something to do with the cab I was driving, like maybe the PUC had condemned it. Or maybe the IRS was after me for never lying on my income tax form. One of the sweetest feelings in the world is reporting all my tips on April 15th. It makes me feel like a demigod—invulnerable, invincible, and completely deluded, which is the best feeling of all.

When I walked into the on-call room at Rocky Cab, Rollo was seated behind the window in the cage eating a donut. I figured he already knew I had been L-2'd and would be grinning with malicious condescension. I had known guys like Rollo in the army. They grinned at me whenever I got called into the CO's office. I gotta be honest though. I used to grin when another dogface got called on the carpet by the Old Man. There was just something funny about getting in trouble in the army because no matter how mad the captain was, you still received your discharge at the end of your enlistment. The army was a lot like high school.

But Rollo wasn't grinning. I immediately began to get worried. Rollo was sort of a barometer of the atmosphere at Rocky Cab, and when Rollo wasn't grinning it worried me.

"Hogan wants to see you right away," he said in a voice so somber that my heart began to sink like mercury or whatever the hell goes up and down inside Torricelli's invention. How could anybody think up a barometer?

I nodded politely at Rollo, walked into the hallway, and climbed the stairs to a door that was closed: Hogan's door.

I knocked three times.

"Come in," Hogan said.

My mercury hit bottom. Hogan usually says "Yeah" when you knock on his door, like he has no interest in talking to anybody on the planet. I get along well with Hogan.

I pushed the door open, and my barometer broke, because two men were present in Hogan's office and I recognized them. Their names were Duncan and Argyle. They were detectives with the Denver Police Department.

CHAPTER 15

"Thanks for coming in, Murph," Hogan said, as he stood up from his desk.

Duncan and Argyle had been seated on folding chairs, but they both stood up when I entered.

"Mister Murphy," Duncan said with a nod. He remembered me. Cops are like that. But he didn't know that I hated being called "Mister Murphy." I hated it because it made me sound like Ensign Parker.

I walked up to the desk. It had been a long time since the three of us had spoken. Not long enough. The first time we had met, these two bloodhounds suspected me of kidnapping and murdering that eighteen-year-old girl. I won't bore you with the details, except to say that they were mistaken. No reflection on the DPD of course, although it does say something positive about my character I suppose.

"I don't believe I need to introduce you gentlemen," Hogan said.

All three of us quickly shook our heads no. I liked that.

"Have a seat, Murph," Hogan said. "Detectives Duncan and Argyle have a missing-person case they're working on and they want to ask you a few questions."

I sat down baffled. That was not unusual. I noticed a number of items on Hogan's desk, including three trip-sheets. I knew right away who they belonged to. I have the unique ability to recognize my own handwriting.

The last time I had spoken with Duncan and Argyle they had remained standing while they interrogated me. In fact I would say they "hovered." But this time they drew up folding chairs and sat on either side of me. The atmosphere was lighter than it had been during the missing girl case. I don't know why people always think of me when girls turn up missing.

"I know you're a busy man, Mister Murphy," Duncan said, "so we'll try to make this short and let you get back on the road."

I lifted my chin and simultaneously raised an index finger. I do this to let people know that I want to say something. By "people" I mean cops. "Please, sir ... call me Murph."

He stuck out a lower lip and nodded. Lower lips are one of the most expressive parts of the human body, next to fingers.

"It's this way, Murph," Duncan said. "We received a report yesterday about a missing man, and we believe he may have been in your taxi some time during the past week."

I felt a flood of relief. Duncan wasn't glaring at me. The glare has the lower lip beat all hollow.

I raised my chin higher. "I understand," I said, which I didn't, but I was "going with the flow."

Argyle reached out and picked up my trip-sheets. He held them up for me to see.

"Mister Hogan here was kind enough to pull your driving records from the files," he said. "Now according to your handwritten account, last Monday you picked up a man at eight-fourteen Tremont."

A chill crept up my spine. My heart skipped a beat. I don't want to get grotesque here, but it reminded me of my first kiss. I knew right away who they were talking about: Trowbridge. Argyle didn't have to show me my other trip-sheets. I could have told him what he was going to say next: "You dropped him off at five-sixteen Curtis Street."

I nodded.

"A few days later you picked him up at five-sixteen Curtis," Duncan interjected from my left side, "and took him to seventeen hundred east Nineteenth."

I nodded. I began to feel a bit "uptight" as the hippies used to say. "That's right, sirs," I said.

The cops glanced at each other. "I mean 'sir,'" I said.

Why did I use the plural? It only made me sound suspicious. I felt like I was in Latin class being hounded by a nun who insisted that my direct object agree with my predicate. I was starting to sweat.

"Now according to this last sheet, you picked up the same fare at seventeen hundred east Nineteenth and dropped him off at Twentieth and Broadway. Is that correct?"

"Yes sir."

"Do you remember the fare's name?" Argyle said.

"Yes sir. His name was Trowbridge."

Argyle softly set the trip-sheet down on the desk and looked me in the eye. He didn't say anything right away. I held his gaze. I knew how to do that. I'd had plenty of experience with authority figures in the army. One thing I had learned in the army was that officer eyes are different from sergeant eyes. Argyle had officer eyes. Briefly—officer eyes are scarier, but let's move on.

"The distance from seventeen hundred east Nineteenth to Broadway and Twentieth is less than two miles," Argyle said. "But according to the time recorded on your trip-sheet," Duncan said, "that two-mile trip took more than an hour."

I looked back and forth, and realized what they were doing. They were playing annoying-cop/annoying-cop.

"Yes sir, that's true," I said. "But I didn't take Mister Trowbridge to the Twentieth Street address right away."

They glanced at each other.

"Where did you take him?" Argyle said.

"To Buffalo Bill's grave," I said, before I could stop myself. Their eyeballs practically collided in mid-air.

Symbolism. I swear to God it's more dangerous than metaphor. I quickly elaborated on my statement.

"Mr. Trowbridge asked me to drive him to the top of Lookout Mountain where Buffalo Bill Cody is buried. That's located out by Golden."

The cops nodded. They knew their territory. They came with it. "So we drove out there," I said. "But after we got halfway up the mountain I pulled off at one of those scenic overlooks?" I said with a questioning lilt at the end of my sentence indicating that I wanted them to acknowledge that they both knew what a scenic overlook was. They did. They nodded and glanced at each other. They were like synchronized swimmers.

"Why did you do that?" Duncan said.

I opened my mouth to reply, and only then did I realize that I didn't quite know how to phrase it. I felt that I understood what had motivated Trowbridge to ask me to pull over—he wanted to take a look at a place on the mountainside that held a nostalgic significance for him, wanted momentarily to reach into his past and grab a handful of something that had compounded the simple joys of a carefree boyhood when he had ranged across his world oblivious to the burgeoning responsibilities and heartbreaks of impending adulthood. But that seemed like a complicated explanation to offer a couple of men who doubtless viewed the world in terms of black and white, of good and evil, and didn't give a tinker's damn for the subtleties of an East Coast college professor's touchy-feely mumbo-jumbo. Consequently I said, "I ... I ... I ... I ... what I mean is ... he asked me to."

The cops glanced at each other. They were good. Esther Williams would have been proud of them. I was floundering. "Why did he do that?" Duncan said.

"He wanted to get out and take a look around. He told me he used to ride his bike up there with his friends when he was a kid."

"He rode a bicycle up Lookout Mountain?"

"Yes."

"Why?"

"Because the downward journey was so much fun." They glanced at each other.

"That's what Trowbridge told me anyway," I said. "He and his friends liked to coast down the road."

"A lot of work for a cheap thrill," Argyle said. I nodded.

"How long were you there?" Duncan said.

"About five minutes."

"What time did you get to the top of the mountain?"

"We didn't get to the top."

"Why not?"

"Trowbridge changed his mind." They glanced at each other. Maybe I'll just say "Glance" from now on.

"Why did he change his mind?" Duncan said.

It was James Dickey all over again. It seemed like people were always asking me to explain why somebody else did something inexplicable. By "people" I mean cops.

"I … don't … know," Jon Voight said.

"What did you do then?" Argyle said.

"What do you mean?"

"After you left the scenic point, where did you go?"

"I drove him back to Denver and dropped him off at …" then I paused.

Glance.

"I dropped him off a few blocks away from Twentieth and Broadway," I said quickly.

Glance.

Argyle picked up the trip-sheet and looked at it for a moment, then set it down. "Your record indicates that you dropped him off at the men's mission on Broadway."

I took a deep breath and nodded. "That's true. That's what it says. But I didn't drop him there."

"Why did you write it down here?"

Because that's what cabbies do, I wanted to say, but didn't. Sometimes we cabbies use a kind of shorthand when filling out trip-sheets. Sometimes we indicate the nearest intersection rather than an exact location for drop-offs, especially if someone wants out in the middle of a block. It makes for easier paperwork. I began to feel even more uptight because a cabbie is supposed to fill out trip-sheets with exactitude ... and because I was talking to cops.

"I wrote it because that's where he eventually went," I said.

"Did he tell you he was going to go to the men's mission?" Argyle said.

"No."

"Then how do you know he went there?"

I sat with my mouth open for a moment, trying to decide how adversely the truth might affect my immediate future. I couldn't make the calculation. I opted to go with the facts. That sometimes works.

"Because after he got out of my cab I followed him there."

Glance.

"Why did you do that?"

From somewhere deep inside me a chortle began to well up. I could sense that things were beginning to careen out of control. I felt like an Anglish comic in a music hall skit. How could I possibly explain to cops how my mind works?

"Because I was concerned about him," I said. "He seemed sort of depressed. He had moved from three different addresses in the past week or so, and I just had the feeling that he was ... you know ... despondent or something."

"Despondent?"

"Yeah. I kind of felt sorry for the guy."

"Do you often feel sorry for people?"

"Yes."

"Why is that?"

"I was raised Catholic," I said. "We're trained to do that."

I could tell they wanted to glance at each other, but they reined it in. I wrote it off as separation of church and state.

"So you followed him to the men's mission," Duncan stated.

"That's right."

"What did you do then?"

"I drove to the Brown Palace Hotel and picked up a fare."

Argyle lifted the trip-sheet and looked at it.

"Who did you pick up?"

"A rich woman."

"How did you know she was rich?"

"She made me nervous."

"Where did you take her?"

"To the Cherry Creek Shopping Center."

He set the trip-sheet down. He reached across Hogan's desk and picked up a small piece of paper. It was a Rocky Mountain Taxicab customer receipt. He held it up so I could see it.

"Did you sign this?" he said.

I stared at my signature. I stared at the date. I stared at the empty space where the cost of the ride was supposed to have been filled in. But mostly I stared at the tiny cramped words that said: "You must not hold a job that you like."

CHAPTER 16

"Yes," I said. I tried not to look at Hogan. I succeeded.

"Did you give this receipt to Mr. Trowbridge?" Argyle said.

"Yes."

"Why isn't the cost of the fare filled in?"

I raised my right hand and let it sort of flap for a moment. Then I lowered it. "The fare came to forty-five dollars, but when I offered him a receipt he said he didn't need one."

"But you gave him this receipt anyway?"

"Yes."

"Why?"

I swallowed hard, the worst thing you can do in front of a detective.

"It was already filled out," I said. "Or filled in. I don't know why the English language has to be so wishy-washy. I mean 'out' is the opposite of 'in.' But anyway, since I already wrote something on it, I just handed it to him."

This time they glanced at Hogan. So did I. I didn't like what I saw. I glanced away.

Argyle nodded. He turned the card around so he could examine it. "There's something we'd like to ask you," he said.

That struck me as an odd statement at this point in the interrogation, but I "went with the flow."

"All right," I said.

"Do you have any idea why Mr. Trowbridge wrote this sentence on your receipt?"

He turned the card around so I could see my own words again, and suddenly I remembered a phrase I first heard in the army: "Never volunteer." I sat there silently staring at the words and wondering why I had ever left Wichita. If Mary Margaret Flaherty had said yes to me I would probably be a wealthy businessman by now and a deacon at Blessed Virgin Catholic Church. Or does the church have deacons? I was never very clear on that. I never even understood what a warrant officer was in the army.

Rather than replying to the question—which is to say, rather than telling the truth—I cleared my throat and tried to collect my thoughts. That didn't work, so I said, "If I may ask, why are you asking me these questions?"

The two men eased back a bit in their chairs, and Duncan gave up a small smile. By "small smile" I mean "cop smile."

"The minister who runs the men's mission called us yesterday and told us that he was afraid Mr. Trowbridge had committed suicide," Duncan said. "Among his belongings we found this receipt with your name on it. That's why we're here."

"But … why does he think Mr. Trowbridge committed suicide?" I said.

"Because he left a suicide note," Argyle said. "We compared the handwriting on your receipt with his note. It matches."

My ego quivered with pleasure. My handwriting had fooled them. Here I was lying to cops through omission, and my ego was dancing with a top hat and cane. I don't think my ego has ever given a damn about me, the bastard.

"Can you tell us exactly what made you think Mr. Trowbridge seemed despondent?" Duncan said. "Was it something he said or did?"

I stared at Duncan. I began to hear a faraway ringing in my ears. This happens whenever reality intrudes upon my life, which doesn't happen very often, but often enough for me to recognize the warning signals.

"He spoke in a dejected tone of voice," I said.

"How do you mean?"

"On the ride to Lookout Mountain he kept talking about his child-hood in a voice that I would describe as 'glum.'"

Duncan nodded. "During the trip, did you get the impression that he might be contemplating suicide?"

I froze.

How could I explain to him that I get that impression from half the people who ride in my backseat?

"It didn't really occur to me," I said. "I simply got the impression that he was taking a trip down memory lane."

"In a taxicab?" Argyle said.

"Yes."

"Expensive trip."

"Yeah," I said. "He was pretty old."

Argyle nodded. He himself looked to be about thirty-five. So did Duncan. All army officers below the rank of colonel always looked thirty-five to me. The army keeps a man physically fit. That's one of the multiple reasons I didn't reenlist.

"Okay, I think we're about finished here," Duncan said. "Thank you for taking time out from your job to talk to us Mister ... I mean Murph."

"Yes ... thanks, Murph," Argyle said.

"Any time," I lied.

They stood up.

Right at that moment there was nothing I wanted more in life than to stand up with them, but I knew it wasn't time for me to stand up. My face was practically sunburned by now. Hogan had been staring at me for the past fifteen minutes. Taxi supervisor eyes are the scariest eyes of all.

Hogan stood up. He told the two detectives that he was glad to have been able to help out. He wasn't lying, I could tell. The DPD and the RMTC have a good relationship, as do all law-enforcement agencies and cab companies. Cops and cabbies have a few things in common, like two-way radios, and danger. But the radio is best.

I sat in the chair while Duncan and Argyle said their goodbyes and walked out the door. After they shut the door, Hogan sat down at his desk and looked at me.

"Are you still here?" he said.

I was gone in sixty seconds, down the stairs and out the door and back on the road, breathing heavily and gripping the steering wheel and telling myself that if I ever caught myself getting involved in the personal lives of my fares again I would … but then it hit me: Trowbridge was dead.

I stopped thinking about myself for the first time in forty-five years and glanced in the rear-view mirror where Trowbridge had been seated three times.

Suicide note.

My handwriting had perfectly matched the handwriting of a man who had written a suicide note. I thought of the first fiver that Trowbridge had given me: "You must wake up each day in a state of total despair."

I thought about the other messages he had written. Then I thought about the message I had written to him on the taxi receipt. That nearly brought my day to an end. What if he had read it and felt he was being ridiculed? In other words, what if he thought like me?

At that moment I experienced a brand of guilt that I had never experienced in my life. For lack of a better phrase I would call it "actual guilt." This is kind of hard to explain, but basically I had always found it difficult to feel guilty about anything I did—meaning activities that normal people would feel guilty about—because I rarely took anything seriously. But suicide?

I felt like turning in my cab for the day and going back to my crow's nest. Then I thought of tracking down Big Al and telling him about these things. But I already knew what he would say. First he would admonish me for getting involved in the personal life of a fare. Then he would convict me for driving a man to suicide. Then he would order me to go to a grotto and dwell on my sins. Finally he would give me my penance, whatever that amounted to. That's what stopped me from tracking down Big Al. He had graduated from a Jesuit high school. The difference between a regular Catholic education and a Jesuit education is the difference between the army and the marines.

Instead, I decided to take refuge in work. I knew a lot of people who had real jobs, and more than once I had heard them say that work is a form of refuge. I never really knew what they meant by that because for me work had always been like jail. I suppose that, technically speaking, a jail might be viewed as a form of refuge—Henry David Thoreau probably viewed it that way, but I decided to give it a try anyway.

Rather than sit outside the hotels the rest of the day, I worked the radio, jumping bells and keeping busy so I wouldn't have to think about the ghost of Mr. Trowbridge, whom I imagined sitting in the backseat. But whenever I glanced into my rear-view mirror, I saw only people going to DIA or Cherry Creek or Union Station or the Denver Tech Center, and not Trowbridge's face superimposed over the faces of any men or women or teenagers or pets. I sometimes get pets in my cab, usually dogs. We're supposed to charge an extra fifty cents for pets, which is about the most cretinous rule I ever heard in my life—although that doesn't include seeing-eye dogs. Seeing-eye dogs have it made.

My plan didn't work very well. Every time a fare climbed out of my cab, my mind went back to thinking about Trowbridge and his glum voice. By five-thirty that evening I had earned back my lease payment and gas and Twinkies, and had made a profit of forty-five dollars. When I counted the forty-five, something caught in my throat. It was the same amount as the ride to Lookout Mountain. It was the same amount I had earned on the first day I met Trowbridge, after excluding his crispy from my profits.

It was a sign from God. I recognized it. He was telling me to go home. Sweeney often gives me this sign around midnight on Saturdays. My friends do, too, mostly at parties, although they simply say it out loud. They don't mess with symbolism.

By six o'clock that evening I was back in my crow's nest lethargically chewing on a burger and sipping a beer and staring at the gray/green screen of my TV. There was no sound and no picture. I couldn't face Mary Ann. After I finished supper and did the dish, I went into the living room and pulled out *The Stranger* and removed the fivers and held them in my hand. They felt like blood money. The messages were the second to the last things that Trowbridge had ever written in his life, and suddenly I wanted them out of my life.

I thought about throwing them away, but that seemed sacrilegious. I had thrown away money before, mostly at the dog track, but throwing away Trowbridge's final words was too unsettling. Then I thought about driving down to the men's mission and putting them into the donation box, but that seemed too little, too late, and too obvious. I thought about simply spending them as if they were normal fivers, but …

I didn't know what to do with them. Then a line of poetry came to mind. It was from an epic poem I had been forced to memorize in high school. "…With my crossbow, I shot the albatross." This occurs to me about three times a year, so there was nothing unusual about it. Then I started thinking about Albert Camus.

Didn't he write a book about suicide?

Of course he did. I read it when I was a junior at the University of Colorado at Denver. It was assigned in a class on European literature. It was called *The Myth of Sisyphus.* I quickly scoured my bookshelves but did not see it anywhere. It was a nonfiction book, which may explain why it had disappeared. I mostly read novels and biographies. Essays don't interest me much. I may have loaned the book to someone and forgotten about it. But I tried to remember—what was it he said? I did recall that he was opposed to the concept of suicide, but on what grounds? It had something to do with the meaninglessness of existence.

I sat down in my easy chair and clutched the fivers in one hand and *L'Étranger* in the other, closed my eyes, and mentally drifted back to my UCD days. I overshot my goal and saw myself naked inside a taxi. The driver was asking how I intended to pay for the trip back to the campus, which I felt was an irrelevant question. From my point of view he was missing The Big Picture.

"I left my money in my pants," I slurred drunkenly.

"Yeah," he said, "but where are your pants?"

He had me over a barrel.

But all that had taken place in Wichita. I drifted forward in time to my student days at UCD, to a literature class, and tried to recall the Camus lecture given by a female teacher whose psychotic love of Henry James had resulted in my getting a D on a sarcastic theme paper about *The Turn of the Screw*, but let's not get into that.

I had a hard time remembering what the teacher had said about Camus because I never paid any attention to the English teachers in college. The only reason I majored in English was because the government was paying for my education, and I figured studying English literature would help in my quest to become a novelist. End result? I drive a cab for a living.

But then it came to me. Camus said that it was irrational to commit suicide based on the premise that life is meaningless, because that would imbue the act of suicide itself with a significance that already has been voided by the assertion that any act is meaningless. Was that it? That was the best I could come up with: a study in circular illogic. I interpreted it to mean that you had to come up with a better reason to commit suicide than meaninglessness. Hell, I could fill a notebook.

So Camus was no help as usual. I did remember my teacher saying that Camus' death was absurd. He survived WWII and the Nazi occupation of France, only to die in a traffic accident at the age of forty-six. I would be forty-six in a year. I stopped thinking about Camus. I turned on the TV and looked at a James Bond movie for a few minutes. I would never see thirty-seven again.

I went into the bedroom, turned off the light, kicked off my Keds and collapsed into bed. And then as I was drifting off to sleep a thought occurred to me: If suicide is the only answer, find a different question.

CHAPTER 17

I woke up the next day in a state of total despair. I lay in bed gazing at the ceiling for ten minutes, then decided it might be best to go to Rocky Cab. This would have been my regularly scheduled day off, or "spring break" as I like to call it, but I wanted to immerse myself in work again. I also wanted to remove the fivers from my life.

I finally decided that the only decent way to get rid of them would be to palm them off onto customers as if I was performing a kind of burial ritual, like the passing of a torch, or scattering ashes above Lake Huron from the open door of a chopper. Maybe "setting them adrift on the asphalt river" would be the best way to describe my approach to getting rid of the albatross feathers. I had never cared much for rituals of any sort, especially the kind where you got sworn into an army, but I could see how the performance of rituals helps people to deal with trauma. Okay. I'll admit it. I heard a self-help guru say that on TV. But since it was on TV, I figured there must be something to it.

I took the fivers out of my Camus and tucked them into my shirt pocket along with my starting money. I always have about twenty dollars in change when I start the day. Sometimes in the morning a first fare will hand me a twenty-dollar bill for a two-dollar trip, which forces me to go to a 7-11 later and try to talk the clerk into exchanging the twenty for small change. I usually end up having to buy a Twinkie. It gets embarrassing. Cabbies and 7-11 clerks have a lot in common, and dealing with twenties is one of them. A lot of 7-11 clerks that I know are ex-cabbies. We switch horses in midstream rather easily.

I was feeling pretty low when I left my crow's nest, thinking about Trowbridge, and about working on a Tuesday, and about palming off burial bucks. Bad things come in threes they say, and I guess sometimes "they" are right. I felt sort of lightheaded that morning, like I was going through the motions of living. This was the same feeling I used to get when I had real jobs that I was required to go to or else get fired. So forcing myself to go to work that day was like being my own supervisor, which left a bad taste in my mouth. I rarely make myself do anything, and if I can think up an excuse for not doing it, I usually fall for it.

I arrived at Rocky Cab at ten minutes till seven. I got out of my heap and carried my plastic briefcase into the on-call room. There were a lot of drivers in there, old pros as well as newbies. Tuesday is the most innocuous day of the week in the world of cab driving, and maybe the world in general. Friday is eons away, and everyone has already gotten over the horror of Monday. I took my place at the end of the short line of drivers waiting their turn at the cage. When my turn came I stepped up to the window and slapped down seventy bucks for a lease.

Rollo didn't say anything. I tried to read his face. It was like trying to read *Peyton Place*. It sickened me. But I couldn't tell if he knew what I had been grilled about in Hogan's office the day before. And I didn't want to know. The less I know about Rollo, etc.

I took my trip-sheet and key to 123 and walked out to the parking lot. As I've stated, 123 was a virtual wreck on the outside, which was how I felt on the inside. Somehow, as I climbed in and got settled, this identification with a wreck seemed to counter the negative feelings inside me, as though two wrecks make a right. I've always said that a taxicab is a terrible place to have an epiphany, yet I couldn't help but feel I was having one. To start the engine, to put the shift into gear, to guide this mess out of the parking lot and onto the mean streets of Denver gave me the feeling that I was guiding not merely a motor vehicle, but my own life.

A strange sense of peacefulness came over me. I had long ago accepted the fact that it was cab driving or nothing in my life, because there was no other job that I could do. Whether I won the lottery or published a bestseller was up to the gods. But this—this thing I was doing—guiding a physical manifestation of my very soul toward a 7-11 store gave me a sense of completeness that I had not experienced since I had received my discharge from the army.

By the time I got 123 parked at the 7-11 gas pump I was feeling the sensation that the self-help gurus refer to as "an inner calm." All of my depression and anxieties seemed to have left me. I'm not saying that they were replaced by a sensation of exhilaration or glee, I simply felt the absence of negative feelings. I went into the store to pay for a tank of gas and a couple of Twinkies, and got in line behind three people, one of whom was trying to return a carton of milk that he had purchased the day before.

"This crap's curdled!" he said.

"You have to show me a receipt," the clerk said. He was a new clerk. I didn't recognize him.

"Who the hell keeps 7-11 receipts!" the guy barked.

Normally any sort of problem in a 7-11 line is enough to ruin my day—a customer trying to cash a third-party personal check, or buy beer without an I.D., or the myriad bizarre things that people do to bring the checkout lanes of America to a grinding halt. I'm sure I don't need to delineate them. You've been there. But as I stood waiting for the logical conclusion of this fruitless ploy to play itself out to the bitter end, I was surprised to find no impatience boiling up inside me. Instead, I felt like I was watching a particularly predictable and mildly amusing episode of a sitcom. It was as if I was not a part of the growing line of customers shuffling and coughing and making those subtle "let's get this show on the road" noises that Americans are so adept at. I felt as if I had all the time in the world—and then I realized I did. I literally had the rest of my life, for this was how my life was always going to be. I had never thought I would experience an epiphany in a 7-11 store, but that's how it felt. I didn't understand what was happening to me. By this point in the confrontation I ought to have been coughing and hacking and sighing, yet I just stood there watching this guy holding up a quart of milk and demanding immediate justice. It sort of made me laugh.

I glanced around and saw the haggard looks on the faces of the customers behind me. There were seven or eight by now. I could sense the combined forces of their frustration traveling up and down the line. If that energy could have been corralled by Oppenheimer during the late 1930s, WWII might never have happened. Yet it bypassed me completely.

The milk man lost. He strode out of the store with the quart clutched in his trembling hands. A man without a receipt hasn't got a chance. I stepped up to the counter and made my purchases. I looked at the clerk's face. I could tell that the confrontation had upset him. My ex-cabbie acquaintances that work at 7-11 stores never get upset. They handle enraged customers with an élan you never see in someone who has just walked out of high school and into the maw of the all-nite kwik-stop mercantile. It's a learned thing.

"That guy was a jerk," I said, but I said it only to let the clerk know that someone was on his side, even if I wasn't. In fact, I had felt that the customer was right. He obviously wasn't pulling a scam. Who would try to return a quart of milk except a person grievously wronged by an expiration date?

The clerk smiled and nodded, then told me that earlier that morning a drunk had staggered into the store, grabbed a six-pack of beer from the cooler, and shouted, "I'm not going to pay for this!" and walked out the door.

"What did you do?" I said.

"Nothing."

"Smart move."

I left the store with my Twinkies clutched like a quart of curdled milk.

Working at a 7-11 is one job I have never considered doing. The clientele is generally the sort I see parading through the backseat of my taxi, so that's no problem, but I've been told what 7-11 clerks do when there are no customers in the store, and it isn't pretty. They stock the shelves with merchandise. All those Twinkies aren't put there by elves. But more significantly, 7-11 clerks have to mop the floor. Need I say more?

The milk vignette at the 7-11 seemed only to enhance the calm I was experiencing as I drove toward the Brown Palace. There was no doubt in my mind now—truly, I held the best of all possible jobs.

When I arrived at the Brown there were four cabs in front of me. My joy increased. I judged it would take forty minutes before I would be first in line, possibly an hour. I was in no hurry. How could a man who had the best of all possible jobs be in a hurry? There was no past and no future in the world I inhabited. There was only the endless present. I began to wonder if the introductory course in Transcendental Meditation that I had attended in college had rubbed off on me and accidentally caused me to become cosmic. What if I had somehow ripped off the Maharishi? Maybe I had become cosmic for free. But I didn't question it. I had learned long ago not to question everything.

I went about getting settled for brunch, opening my Coke and unwrapping a Twinkie, and pulling my paperback from my briefcase. And then, last of all, I pulled my starting cash from my shirt pocket and began arranging and separating the one-dollar bills from the larger bills—and my hair stood on end. Not literally of course, but to hell with creative writing teachers—my Rocky cap bounced off the head liner.

The Trowbridge fivers were missing.

I dug deep, but my pocket was empty. I began searching through my sundry other pockets, trying to remember if I had tucked them into a new place for safekeeping. I even poked through that tiny pocket on my bluejeans that they sew above the right-hand front pocket and that nobody ever uses. Who designed that joke? Strangely, on the rare occasion that I buy a pair of jeans that doesn't have the little pocket, I feel like I'm wearing girl pants. Go figure.

But I couldn't find the fivers anywhere. It was at this point that I received an L-2.

CHAPTER 18

"One twenty-three, one twenty-three, el-two," the dispatcher said. I froze.

The L-2 combined with the missing Trowbridge money made me uneasy.

A horn honked.

I glanced in my rear-view mirror. A Rocky Cab was parked behind me. I squinted my bifocal contacts to see who it was. I feared it might be Big Al. But it was just a newbie. On the surface it may have appeared that he honked in order to let me know that the dispatcher was trying to get a hold of me—a common courtesy—but I knew the real reason: he wanted me to go away so he could move forward one space.

I reached for the microphone. I held it like a fragile egg in my hand. I decided to move to Wichita.

Honk!

I pressed the button, "Check," and released it. My fate was sealed like a baggie.

Actually, I was grateful to the newbie for engaging in behavior that, under other circumstances, might have gotten him a scowl. The incessant honking was like the tolling of a bell that kept me from slipping back into a dreamlike realm of self-delusion so intense that it astonished even me, and I've been writing unpublished novels for twenty years.

I started my engine, put the shift into gear, then made a fake show of having trouble pulling out, which I knew would irritate the newbie. Just because I was grateful didn't mean I had to return the favor.

Let him stew. The line wasn't moving anyway. Tuesdays are terrible at the hotels.

I arrived at Rocky Cab fifteen minutes later. I stuffed my trip-sheet and key into my briefcase, then climbed out with the briefcase in hand. I headed for the on-call room. Rollo was reaching for a donut when I walked in. He glanced at me and his hand froze, his fingertips barely brushing the glaze on his Spudnut. "Spudnut" is a brand of donut made in Denver. It involves a snack truck. It gets complicated.

He drew his hand away from the donut. I had never seen him do this before. It made my skin crawl.

He licked his lips. I saw something like fear in his eyes, which I had never seen before either. I had seen it in other people's eyes, especially in basic training, but I doubted if Rollo had ever done a pushup.

"You better get upstairs," Rollo said. "Hogan wants to see you."

That ringing started up in my ears again. I nodded at Rollo and walked past the cage, entered the hallway, and climbed the stairs to the closed door.

I knocked three times. "Yeah," Hogan said.

That was the okay signal to enter.

I pushed the door open and took one step into the room—and froze. Duncan and Argyle were standing beside the desk. They took one look at me and froze. Hogan froze, too. It was like a scene in a movie where everybody stops moving. I'm thinking "freeze-frame," the laziest special effect ever handed to a director on a silver platter.

Duncan and Argyle suddenly moved. I could tell by their maneuver that they wanted to make sure I didn't back out the door, race down the stairs, hop into my car, and drive to Mexico. I could tell by the way they grabbed my arms.

"Take it easy," Argyle said. "Don't give us any trouble."

"Okay," I said, and let them escort me toward my usual chair.

Argyle took my briefcase away from me, and Duncan pressed on top of my shoulders, causing me to sit down on the chair. It was all very professional. Quick and clean. They knew their business.

A few items were lying on Hogan's desk, but I didn't recognize them.

"I want to advise you of your rights," Duncan said. "Anything you say to us from this point on may be held against you in a court of law."

"I understand," I said. "But like … I mean … am I under arrest?"

"Not yet," Argyle said. He could have been an English major. He was good at foreshadowing.

"We just want to ask you a few questions, Murph," Duncan said. "It has to do with the statements you made to us yesterday."

"All right," I said. After all, I knew I was innocent of breaking any laws, so it seemed okay to me.

Argyle reached into his coat pocket and pulled out a white envelope.

I watched his fingers manipulate the flap. He had cop fingers. They were good. The flap opened fast. He reached inside and withdrew five feathers. They had come from a bird called the albatross.

"Do you recognize these?" he said.

I swallowed harder than I had ever swallowed in my life. Of course I recognized them, but I especially recognized the one with the shortest sentence, the one that I myself had written: the forgery.

"Yes."

"When you arrived at work this morning, did you pay for your taxi lease with these?"

I started to say, "I … don't … know," which was true. But I had the feeling that my definition of truth had more to do with splitting hairs than coming clean. I realized then that I had inadvertently given the fivers to Rollo when I had paid for my lease. But had I given the fivers to Rollo or had my Univac? Had one of us pulled a fast Freudian on me when I handed over that seventy bucks? If so, it could explain why I had felt so calm from the moment I left Rocky Cab, so free, so complacent and content. I had shot the albatross by simply dumping the money without realizing it on a conscious level. I do that often, usually during last-call at Sweeney's, so this situation was not without precedent.

"I guess I must have," I said. "Where did you get them?"

"Rollo turned them in to me," Hogan said. He didn't look happy.

I took a deep breath and heaved a sigh. I sometimes do that when coming clean, so as you might surmise, I don't heave many sighs.

"I got three of them from Mr. Trowbridge," I said.

There was a long pause in the conversation. I could hear the squeak of a fan, and Hogan didn't even have one.

"Where did you get the other two?" Argyle said.

"I got one of them from a bartender."

"What about the last one?"

"I don't remember."

"You don't remember?"

"Well … actually I do remember. I got it from my billfold."

"What do you mean?"

"I mean I removed it from the dollar-bill pocket of my billfold."

"Why did you do that?"

Because I'm insane. "So I could write the words that are on it."

Argyle slowly looked over at Duncan. Duncan nodded. Argyle slipped the bills back inside the envelope and tucked it into his coat pocket. "You told us yesterday that you drove Mr. Trowbridge up Lookout Mountain, is that correct?"

"Yes."

"You said you stopped at a scenic overlook halfway up the mountain, is that correct?"

"Yes."

"Then you drove Mr. Trowbridge back to Denver and let him off a few blocks away from the men's mission, is that correct?"

"Yes."

"Did anybody see you drop him off?"

"I don't know. I suppose. There was traffic."

Glance.

Argyle slowly came around and positioned himself so that he was looking down at me. "Based on the information that you gave us, we sent some men up Lookout Mountain to make a search. We found something on the mountain."

Duncan reached toward the items on Hogan's desk. He held up a wristwatch. "Do you recognize this?"

I nodded. I recognized it after all. It was gold. I had seen it once before. "It looks like the wristwatch Mr. Trowbridge was wearing."

Glance.

Duncan picked up a driver's license and held it up for me to see. I looked at Trowbridge's photograph. It was the worst driver's license photo I had ever seen in my life.

Then Duncan showed me two credit cards. Both of them belonged to Trowbridge. "Our men found these at the base of the cliff," he said.

That's all he said.

The silence in the office was unnerving.

Argyle broke it. "We have a team of men currently searching the mountainside for Mr. Trowbridge's body."

My gut turned to water. I thought of the automobile wrecks I had seen piled against the evergreens. I thought of Trowbridge's remark about riding off the cliff at thirty miles an hour on his bike. It was a sheer drop for a long way. Nobody could survive a ... jump ... from that height.

"Is that where he did it?" I said.

Glance.

Argyle pulled a chair around and sat facing me directly. "What we would like you to do, Murph, is to describe again in exact detail what you did from the moment you picked up Mr. Trowbridge until the moment you last saw him."

All right now. Okay. I was an English major in college, and one thing I had learned how to do was parse sentences. Maybe the professors had failed to teach me how to write bestselling works of great literature, but they did show me how to strip a sentence to its essentials and leave the parts lying around like rusty screws on my father's tool bench. And that sentence of Argyle's was jam-packed with screws, i.e., "exact detail what YOU did from the moment YOU picked up Mr. Trowbridge until the moment YOU last saw him."

I didn't give a tinker's damn who was watching. I swallowed hard. Then I recalled something that my Maw used to say to me when I was a kid: "The truth will set you free, unless you're guilty."

I took a deep breath and looked Argyle right in the eye. I proceeded to tell him every last detail that I could remember about my trip halfway up to Buffalo Bill's grave. Duncan was busy taking notes, and he wasn't being the least bit discreet about it. Argyle listened to my narrative with his eyes fixed on mine. I don't think he blinked more than twice during the fifteen minutes I spoke. I became so fascinated by this that I started speaking more slowly just to see how long it would take between blinks. Then I started thinking about a movie I once saw where a character painted eyeballs on his eyelids so he could sleep while appearing to be awake. It was either Douglas Fairbanks, Sr. or Red Skelton. I couldn't remember. I was too busy describing the journey up Lookout Mountain. By now Trowbridge and I were standing at the apex of the scenic overlook.

"Trowbridge slapped his hand on one of the abutments and said it was the same one where he always sat when he was a kid. He said he would drink a soda and wait for the stragglers to arrive."

Duncan jotted a note. Whenever he wrote something, his pen made a sound like this: "skritch, skritch." I don't suppose I have to tell you that it was getting on my nerves. I won't bring it up again.

Even though I had already described this scene to Duncan and Argyle, I did the repeat performance without complaint. I was determined to let them know by my tone of voice and my body language that I was willing to cooperate to the best of my ability, for I had no doubt that these officers possessed their own brand of mental Univac which allowed them to make quick and accurate judgments about suspects, criminals, and me.

"Then Trowbridge pointed out the car wrecks at the bottom of the cliff," I said. "I leaned over and took a look, and I didn't like what I saw. That's when I decided it was time to …"

And I stopped.

I stared at Argyle's dilated pupils.

The reason I stopped was because I suddenly recalled something that I hadn't said to the two men the day before, something that I had even denied after a fashion.

Duncan stopped writing on his pad. Glance.

"You decided it was time to do what?" Argyle said.

That's when I realized I had stopped at the wrong point in my narrative. At best I never should have started the sentence. Second-best would have been to complete it. But no, I had to end the sentence with "decided it was time to …" The abrupt cessation of speech made it sound like I was hiding something. I didn't even need to see it in their eyes, which I could. I always know whenever it looks like I'm hiding something from somebody. I've gotten good at hiding things over the years, but I haven't perfected it yet. However, I do know a faux pas when I hear one. Like the next one for instance.

CHAPTER 19

I chortled. This is a problem that I frequently suffer from: objectivity. When I find myself in a situation that could objectively be described as "ludicrous," I often chortle as though I were viewing myself as a character in a movie. Specifically, a comedy. Like a member of a theater audience watching Laurel and Hardy walking inattentively toward an open manhole, I start laughing before anything funny has actually happened. The problem is that in real life, laughing inexplicably can be unnerving to nearby people, such as bus passengers, bank customers, and cops.

"No … what I mean is … I just remembered something," I said, dropping my smile.

Glance.

"You were saying that it was time to what?" Argyle said.

"Yeah. Time to … what?" Duncan said.

"I was going to say it was time to … to get in my cab and go on up the mountain. But I just now remembered something that I forgot to tell you yesterday."

Glance. Glance. Glance.

Duncan and Argyle kept looking from each other to me and back to each other again. They were like kittens watching a ping-pong game.

I kept talking. "I didn't want to look at the wrecks, so I walked back toward my cab. But when I turned around to see if Trowbridge was following me, he was kneeling on the abutment."

"What do you mean?" Argyle said.

"I mean he had crawled up onto the stone wall. He was on his hands and knees looking out over the edge of the cliff."

Glance.

I think I'll knock off the "Glance" business from now on. You probably have the general idea about Duncan and Argyle's synchronized-swimming approach to investigative teamwork.

"Why didn't you tell us this yesterday?" Duncan said.

I started to say "I … don't … know," but one Jon Voight per fine mess was my limit. Instead I said, "I just didn't think of it. That's what I meant when I abruptly ceased speaking a moment ago. Yesterday you asked me if Trowbridge said or did anything that might indicate to me that he was thinking of committing suicide. Well, the fact is, for a moment there I thought he was going to jump off the cliff."

I'm sorry. I gotta do this one more time. Glance.

Okay. End of gimmick.

The cops peered at me. Let's be frank. I was fully aware by now that they suspected me of bumping off Mr. Trowbridge.

And then, in a voice that was so soft and steady and slow that he might have been painting Fabergé eggs with his breath, Argyle said, "Did he make a move to jump?"

"No he didn't," I said in a similar voice. This is another problem I have. I start talking like the people who are talking to me. It's a cabbie habit. It's motivated by tips, i.e., you don't want to start talking like Abbie Hoffman if General Patton is in your backseat. But the habit becomes so ingrained that you sometimes forget that tipping doesn't take place "outside the cab," which is to say, no lawman ever handed me a tip at the end of a grilling.

"What did he do next?" Duncan said.

"He didn't do anything. He just kept kneeling there. I told him I had left the meter running, but he didn't move. So I went back toward him."

"Why?"

"Because ... like I said ... I had this idea that he was going to jump. I kind of started walking fast. And then ..."

I stopped.

"And then ... what?" Argyle said.

I couldn't stop myself from stopping at the wrong places in the middles of sentences. It happened every time I started thinking. Thank God I wasn't chewing gum.

"I walked toward Mr. Trowbridge with my arms out."

"Out how?"

"Well ... like this," I said, and I reached toward my supervisor, Hogan. That was mere coincidence. Or was it?

"Why did you do that?"

"Because I had the feeling he was going to jump and so did my arms. I mean, it was instinctive. Before I even got to him I thought I was going to have to grab him."

Argyle sat up straight and said, "How fast were you moving?"

"I would say that I was moving at a quick shuffle."

"What do you mean?"

"Fast ... but not running."

"That sounds like a trot."

"It wasn't quite a trot. I guess it was more of a lope."

"So you were loping toward Mr. Trowbridge with your arms sticking straight out in front of you, is that correct?"

"Well ... my elbows were poised in a slight crook."

"Crook?"

"Bent at the joints."

I crooked my elbows to demonstrate.

"Then what happened?" Duncan said.

I paused and lifted my eyes to a point above Hogan's head. Argyle glanced around at the wall. "What are you looking at, Murph?"

I lowered my eyes and looked at Argyle. "I'm trying to picture the scene in my mind so I can describe it accurately. I often do this when I'm writing prose fiction. It's a tip I once read in a how-to book."

"Fiction?" he said.

"Novels," I said.

"What kind of novels do you write?"

"Unpublished."

Argyle looked at Duncan. It wasn't a glance. It was more of a telepathic inquiry. I recognized it. I once wrote a novel about two telepaths who robbed a bank.

"Do you enjoy making up stories, Murph?"

I swallowed hard. "Well ... 'enjoy' may not be the right word. I've been doing it for twenty years, and while I did enjoy it when I started writing in college, the thrill sort of wore off after fifteen years. Rejection slips had a lot to do with it. Nowadays I think of writing as hard work rather than the lark it was when I was a student and felt that writing a novel was merely a matter of getting some words down on paper and ... and ..."

I stopped talking again. I had the feeling I had either answered the question or hadn't come close.

"Excuse me, gentlemen," Hogan said. "I'm sorry to interrupt, but approximately thirty-four percent of the drivers at Rocky Cab are unpublished writers. You can check my files."

Argyle nodded. "No need, Mr. Hogan. I'll take your word for it. Half the lab boys in Homicide are writing techno-thrillers."

He turned back to me. "When you approached Mr. Trowbridge with your arms crooked, did you take hold of him?"

"No, sir. He climbed down off the abutment before I actually reached him."

"So you didn't touch him?"

"No, sir."

"Did you tell him that you were afraid he was going to jump?"

"No."

"Why not?"

"I would have been embarrassed."

"Why is that?"

"I don't like people to know I think things."

"What happened after the incident ended?"

"We got back into my cab, then he told me he had changed his mind and wanted to return to Denver."

"Why did he change his mind?"

James Dickey was back. I decided to try a new way of phrasing my reply. "I … didn't … ask."

"Why not?"

"I never ask my customers why they go places. I just take them there."

"Let me see if I have this straight," Duncan said, referring to his notebook. "Mr. Trowbridge asked you to take him to the top of Lookout Mountain. You stopped at a scenic overview halfway up, got out, and looked over the cliff. Mr. Trowbridge climbed onto an abutment and looked over the edge, and you loped toward him with your arms out because you were afraid he was going to jump. Is that correct?"

"Yes."

"And then, after the two of you got back into the cab, Mr. Trowbridge inexplicably changed his mind about going to the top, and he asked you to take him back to Denver. Is that correct?"

For a moment I was tempted to joust with Duncan over the word "inexplicably." But I had to remind myself that I was no longer in college where debating the nuances of language couldn't get you arrested.

"Yes."

"Then you drove him back to Denver and dropped him off in an area where there may or may not have been any witnesses."

"Yes."

Duncan closed his notebook and looked at his partner.

"I think we had better continue this conversation down at head-quarters."

I waited for the cuffs to come out.

I had a long wait. I wasn't under arrest. Not yet anyway. Duncan told me that they just wanted to take me in for some further questioning. He said things were getting a little murky. I knew what he was referring to. He was referring to me.

I stood up and reached for my briefcase, but Duncan said he would hold onto it for the time being. As the detectives accompanied me down the stairs and out to their unmarked car, I felt ashamed. Nobody in my family had ever been "taken in for questioning." Whenever the cops showed up at the Murphy house, they always had a bona fide arrest warrant. One of my uncles, Kenneth Murphy, was arrested in Tennessee in 1950. It was during the trial of Julius and Ethel Rosenberg. Uncle Ken had been a janitor at Oak Ridge, but let's drop it. The federal government did, for lack of evidence.

They drove me to DPD. I had taken fares there before but I had never been inside. It was a newish building that covered the entire block between 13th and 14th at Bannock. Slick architecture. Vast apron of concrete that you had to cross to get to the front door, except we went in the back door, i.e., the basement entrance. It was a basement like all basements. I could have designed that basement.

Architects.

Give me a break.

We took an elevator up to Missing Persons. I wondered why they didn't call it "Missing People." What's the difference between Persons and People? I decided not to ask. I had the feeling Duncan and Argyle were in no mood for etymology.

"Have a seat, Murph," Duncan said.

We were in a small room. If you've ever seen *In Cold Blood*, you've seen a small room.

I sat on a chair by a table. It was the same table you see in all small rooms. Rectangular. Wooden. Big enough for two cops to sit side-by-side opposite me. There was only one thing missing: an ashtray. The state had outlawed smoking in government buildings. Now only outlaws smoked in government buildings. I used to smoke cigarettes, but that was long ago and in another shirt: white collar.

Duncan and Argyle left me alone in the room. They told me they had some official business to take care of. It may have been a veiled reference to a restroom, but I didn't ask. I sat alone for five minutes, certain that my every move was being recorded by a secret hidden camera. I've felt this way ever since I was six, the same year I entered Blessed Virgin Catholic Grade School. When I was a kid I used to put a towel over the bathroom mirror in our house whenever I used the can because I thought it was a "TV window." I thought all my classmates were watching me through it. But when I went to school everybody acted innocent. This made me even more suspicious.

At any rate, the idea that I was being watched by members of the DPD made me sit very still. I became self-conscious. I became aware of my every physical motion. I tried to act innocent. I knew how to do it. I had twelve years of Catholic schoolmates under my belt. But suddenly it occurred to me that by sitting too still I might look suspicious, so I decided to move around a bit: cough, scratch my nose, blink a few times, scoot my chair back, rub my left elbow, clear my throat, suck in my cheeks, cross my eyes, and wiggle my fingers like a piano player—you get the picture.

Then Duncan and Argyle walked back in.

CHAPTER 20

Argyle was holding a sheet of paper. I looked at it fast and hard, then looked away. It made me wish I had X-ray vision. There's nothing quite as suspenseful as a cop holding a sheet of paper. It's like he's holding your brain.

I had to ask.

"Did they find Mr. Trowbridge's body yet?" Duncan and Argyle glanced at each other.

I might be forced to go back to that "Glance" deal. They did it an awful lot. If I do though, I'll keep it to a minimum. It's too bad cops aren't telepathic. If they were, they wouldn't glance at each other so much, and they would solve a lot more crimes.

By the way—just so you know—my telepathic bank robbers didn't get away with it. Neither did I, and I've got the rejection slips to prove it.

"We're not at liberty to discuss that, Murph," Argyle said.

I nodded. I figured the police had already found the body. In order to show my sympathy, I curled my lips against my teeth, bowed my head, and shook it. When I looked up, I had the feeling they had just finished glancing at each other, but I wasn't sure.

Argyle pulled the envelope from his coat pocket and laid it in the middle of the table along with the sheet of paper. Then he and Duncan sat down opposite me. Duncan opened the envelope and removed the fivers.

"I wonder if you could do us a favor, Murph," Duncan said.

"Anything," I said.

"What we would like you to do is sort out these bills and tell us where you got each one."

"All right," I said.

I rubbed my nose and adjusted my chair, as if I was preparing to take a test. This was a mistake. Me and tests never got along very well. Every time I took a test in grade school I felt like the nun was watching my brain with a secret hidden camera. I immediately began to sweat. I couldn't hear the squeak of a fan, but I was waiting for it. I could see an air vent.

I separated the bills into three stacks. Two of the stacks had only one bill each, if you know what I mean.

Then I proceeded to describe the events that led up to the acquisition of the bills. I won't repeat it here. You've been there. I picked up each bill and described its history. Duncan glanced from the bills to my eyes as I spoke, but Argyle never glanced at the bills. Through the entire account, he never once took his eyes off my eyes. I don't know if he even blinked. He may have done it while I was reading aloud from the bills, but every time I glanced up at him he was meeting my eyes with an unblinking gaze. It reminded me of the times I tried to see my own eyes move in a mirror. Have you ever tried to do that? It can't be done. Crazy, huh?

As I related the tale of each bill, I began to calm down. I felt as if I was merely having a conversation with two friendly policemen. I even felt as if, in a sense, I myself was a policeman, insofar as I was helping out with a missing-persons investigation. That is to say, I felt like I was their equal, doing everything within my power to help keep the bad dudes in check.

"Now this is the most interesting fiver, as far as I'm concerned," I said, pointing at "stack" number two. I read the words on the bill aloud. "You must be prepared at any given moment to relinquish all semblance of dignity."

"Why is that the most interesting bill?" Duncan said.

"This is the one I got in the bar."

"What bar?"

"Sweeney's Tavern."

Duncan nodded. He obviously knew the place. He had probably worked Vice.

"I went into Sweeney's and ordered a beer, and after I sat down at a booth I looked at my change, and I found this fiver. Well … I mean, you can imagine how I felt."

"How did you feel, Murph?" Argyle suddenly said. It was the first time he had spoken since our investigation had recommenced.

"Well … I mean, I was taken aback."

"How's that?"

"Surprised," I said. "Astonished, actually."

"So this is the third bill you received from Mr. Trowbridge?" he said.

"Yes. No. I didn't … I mean, yes, I could see it was obviously Mr. Trowbridge's handwriting, but no, I didn't get it from him. I got it from the bartender."

"What's the bartender's name?"

"Harold. He's a new employee. And just between you and me, he's kind of a twit."

Argyle gave me one of those eyeless cop-smiles: nothing above the lips moved.

Then …"What day was this?" Duncan said.

"The same day my taxi burned up," I said, and I grinned.

Glance.

"What's this about a burning taxi?" Duncan said.

"My taxicab burned up," I said. "In fact, it happened on the same day I took Mr. Trowbridge up Lookout Mountain. A little later that afternoon my taxi caught on fire and completely burned up. After that I went to the bar."

Suddenly the fan came on. It didn't squeak, but it did make a swoosh sound. Duncan and Argyle squinted at each other.

"Your taxicab burned up while you were on duty?" Duncan said.

"Yes."

"So why did you go to a bar?"

I shifted uneasily on my chair, licked my lips, and grinned at Duncan. "I asked myself that very same question after I got to the bar."

"What was your answer?" Argyle said.

"I couldn't come up with one."

"Maybe you'd better."

"I guess I went to the bar because I panicked."

"Why?"

"It's in my nature."

Argyle took a deep breath and sighed. "All right, Murph, tell us about this cab-burning incident. When and how did it happen?"

I picked up the story from the point where I had dropped Trow-bridge off. I told them about the ensuing fares, culminating with my trip down Peña Boulevard and the sudden lurching of 127's engine. I came to the slightly embarrassing part where I decided that rather than pull off the highway I would try to make it to the motor.

"If your engine was stuttering," Argyle said, "why didn't you pull over and park?"

"Because I'm an optimist."

"How do you mean?"

That was the embarrassing part. "Whenever things start verging on the calamitous, I go into a kind of denial trance. I pretend that every-thing will work out fine. I guess 'pretend' is the operative word here."

"Do things usually work out fine?" Argyle said.

"Things never work out fine," I said.

"Then why do you do it?"

"Because I'm an optimist."

I was sort of lying, but not malevolently. I'm not really an optimist. But I always do go into a denial trance when my life takes a nosedive. It's cheaper than visiting a psychiatrist, and the word "optimist" is something that ordinary people understand better than I understand my inability to face reality.

"Didn't you know that you were performing an unsafe driving procedure that might have gotten you in trouble with the law?" Duncan said.

I pursed my lips and nodded. "On a conscious level I was thinking only about making it back to the cab company. But I guess on an unconscious level I knew that what I was doing was ... well ... absurd."

Glance.

"But to be honest with you, Officer Duncan, I've spent my whole life doing absurd things and getting away with them, so it's become second nature to me. I guess I'm like a gambler. Only I don't gamble for money because I have almost no understanding of the complexity of mathematical odds. I prefer to leave things up to chance. The odds of my winning seem better. I mean, I either win or I lose. That's a fifty-fifty chance, right?"

The cops stared at me for awhile, then Argyle said, "Tell us about the burning cab, Murph."

I talked. But I left out the bang bang bang bang part because I was afraid I would start laughing. Or weeping. Either way it wouldn't have looked good.

"So a policeman did arrive to investigate the incident?"

"Yes."

Duncan and Argyle looked at each other. I knew what they were thinking. Somewhere on the mean streets of Denver was a patrolman they wanted to talk to.

"Sweeney's Tavern," Argyle said. "Where does that fit into this story?"

I told them my bar story. I told them everything.

"So you walked away from Rocky Cab around one o'clock in the afternoon, and you returned around three o'clock."

"That's right."

"So there was a two-hour time span between the burning of the cab and your reporting back in."

It took all my willpower not to roll my eyes. I hate it when people ask me to state the obvious. The energy it takes could be better spent watching TV. "That's correct," I said.

"You didn't by any chance stop at your apartment on the way to the bar?"

"I never stop anywhere on my way to a bar."

They stared at me in silence for a moment, then Argyle said, "Did any of your passengers accidentally leave anything in your taxi that day?"

I frowned. "No."

"How do you know?"

I shrugged. "I would have seen it, whatever it was."

"Has anyone ever accidentally left anything in your taxi?"

"It happens all the time."

"Could you give us a for-instance?"

"Well … one time a girl left a purse in my cab that had twelve-hundred dollars in it."

"What did you do with the purse?"

"I tracked her down and gave it back to her."

"Did the police get involved?"

"Yes. You two guys."

They looked at each other. They nodded.

"Tell me something, Murph," Argyle said. "Is it possible that Mr. Trowbridge might have left something in your cab?"

I stared at him blankly. "Possible" was such an open-ended word that I almost felt like laughing. Anything is possible in this three-ring circus we call life.

"No."

"Why not?"

"Because Mr. Trowbridge was carrying two boxes when he got into my cab, and he had them when he got out."

"Is it possible that he might have removed any objects from the boxes and hidden them under the seat?"

"Yes."

"Why do you say that?"

"Because anything is possible in this ... in a cab. I keep my eyes on the road when I drive, so he could have done something like that at some point. But I don't have any reason to think he did."

"Why not?"

"Well ... I just don't, that's all. It sounds like you're asking me to prove a negative, which of course is philosophically impossible."

At this point I began to get the feeling I was starting to lecture these men on the subtleties of Aristotelian logic, but I didn't think that's what they were looking for.

"If Mr. Trowbridge had left something hidden in your taxi, would it have been obliterated by the fire?"

"You better believe it!" I chirped. "There was nothing left of that cab but a charcoal briquette!" I grinned big and chortled.

Argyle picked up the sheet of paper from his desk. "We interviewed the landlords of the apartment buildings where Mr. Trowbridge stayed during the past two weeks, and every one of the landlords told us that Mr. Trowbridge had left behind boxes of personal belongings in his room when he moved out."

"That explains it," I said.

"Explains what?"

"I picked up Mr. Trowbridge three times, and the last two times he had fewer possessions than before. But I just figured he was pawning stuff to get money."

"How much stuff did he have in his possession the first time you saw him?"

"Enough to fill my trunk."

"How much did he have the last time you saw him?"

"Like I said, two small boxes. He was holding them on his lap during our trip up Lookout Mountain."

"Did he have them when he got out of your cab at the end of the trip?"

"Yes. He took them with him. I saw them. He was carrying them when he entered the men's mission."

"Do you know what caused your cab to burn up?"

"Pardon?"

"Do you know what happened to cause your taxicab to catch on fire and burn up?"

"No."

"Why not?"

"I never asked."

"Why not?"

"I decided to let sleeping dogs lie."

"Do you do that often?"

"Yes."

"How often?"

"Always. It's my philosophy of life."

"Weren't you curious to know why your cab caught on fire?"

"Yes."

"Then why didn't you ask about it?"

"I try to keep a leash on my urges."

"Do you always succeed?"

"No."

"Why is that?"

"I'm only human. But I did manage to give up smoking cigarettes fifteen years ago."

I didn't mention the cigars.

Duncan reached out and picked up the third "stack." He held it up for me to see. "Murph," he said, "why did you write this sentence on this five-dollar bill?"

I was afraid he would get around to that.

CHAPTER 21

Before I could answer, Argyle reached into the white envelope and pulled out one last item: the taxi receipt that I had given to Trowbridge. He held it up for me to see.

"The sentence on this five-dollar bill and the sentence on this receipt were written by the same person," he said. "It's the same person who filled out your trip-sheets."

"I know."

"We brought in a handwriting expert to examine both sentences and compare them with the handwriting on your trip-sheets, and the handwriting matches."

"I know."

"Can you explain that?"

"Yes."

"Explain it."

"Because I wrote both sentences."

Argyle set the card down on the table, then sat back in his chair.

"That's not what you told us yesterday," Duncan said.

I looked at him. "I know. But if you recall our conversation, I didn't actually deny it."

"We do recall our conversation, Murph," Argyle said. "You left us with the impression that Mr. Trowbridge had written that sentence on the receipt."

"I know."

"Why did you do that?"

I shrugged. "Sleeping dogs?"

"That's not good enough, Murph."

"I know."

"Try again."

"Try" was the operative word there. I came clean. I told them about my paranoia. I told them I thought that I was being persecuted by Mr. Trowbridge, until I found the third bill in the bar. That was when I realized Trowbridge wasn't targeting me. He was targeting the entire human race. Or at least, that was my take on it.

"What originally made you think Mr. Trowbridge was persecuting you, Murph?"

"Well, frankly I was baffled by it. I had never met him before, so I didn't understand why he would … you know … write these strange messages to me. But I finally realized I must be wrong. I normally never get strange messages from people. At least, not in writing."

"What other kinds of strange messages do you get?"

"I'm referring to phone calls from strangers offering me sweet deals."

"What strangers?"

"Telemarketers. They leave messages on my answering machine all day."

Glance.

"You still haven't told us why you wrote this message on both the receipt and the five-dollar bill."

"When I was a kid I owned a sheltie … wait … let me start over. I wrote the message on the receipt because I was sort of playing a game. I wanted to get Mr. Trowbridge's reaction."

"Why?"

I raised both hands with my palms spread, then let them flop onto my lap. "I was hoping he would notice the message, and then he might explain to me why he kept writing things down on money."

"Did you write the message on the five-dollar bill before or after you wrote it on the receipt?"

"After."

"Why did you do that?"

"Well … I was just idly sitting around in my apartment and I decided to write it on the bill to see how it stacked up against Trowbridge's messages."

"How did it stack up?"

"It seemed kind of thin."

"You managed to match his handwriting well enough to almost fool our handwriting expert," Argyle said. "Were you trying to do that?"

"I wasn't trying to fool anybody. I was just messing around."

"Do you mess around a lot, Murph?"

"Yes."

"Why?"

"Oh … you know … I don't lead a very active life. I get bored, so I mess around."

"But what exactly was your intent when you wrote those words on the bill?"

"I wanted to see how my handwriting looked in comparison to Mr. Trowbridge's."

"But why?"

"Just messing around."

"Don't you like your job, Murph?"

I was so nonplused by this statement that I was rendered speechless. Bad move. I sat there with my mouth open, unable to respond to such a ludicrous suggestion. I loved my job.

Apparently prompted by the fact that I wasn't answering, Argyle picked up another bill and said, "Tell me something, Murph. Do you ever wake up in a state of total despair?"

Duncan leaned toward me. "Do you harbor any shameful secrets in your past, Murph?"

My eyes about popped out of my head.

"Do you feel that you have no dignity?" Argyle said.

And then, from somewhere deep inside me, a bubble of laughter began to form. It was teensy, like the bubbles you see appearing inside a glass of beer. I'll never understand carbonation. How does it get inside a liquid? And why doesn't it come out all at once instead of slowly?

Anyway, that's what the laughter felt like, a tiny bubble in my gut getting bigger and bigger and rising higher and higher toward my throat. I could feel my vocal chords rubbing their hands with anticipation.

Then Argyle said, "Murph, did you in fact write all of these sentences on these five-dollar bills?"

"No!" I said. It was like waking from a dream. Nothing was funny anymore. "I only wrote the sentence about the job, and that's all. I did it just to compare and contrast the form and content. I was once an English major, and that's what English majors do. And I'll tell you something else. I never actually saw Mr. Trowbridge write any of those sentences. For all I know he didn't even write them."

"We matched his handwriting with the suicide note," Argyle said.

"How do you know he wrote the suicide note?" I said. "Maybe I wrote it!"

There was a moment of silence as Duncan and Argyle stared at me. I damn near stared at myself.

"Except I didn't," I said hurriedly. "I'm just trying to point out that nobody knows if Mr. Trowbridge wrote any of those messages. Maybe … maybe …"

Laurel and Hardy were mere inches away from the manhole. I started laughing.

Glance.

"We have other samples of Mr. Trowbridge's handwriting," Duncan said quietly. "Papers from the boxes he left in the apartments. We have no doubt that he wrote the suicide note."

It was as if Buster Keaton had risen out of the manhole just in time for Stan Laurel to step on his head and continue down the street. "Well … okay," I said, shaking my head sideways like a rattle. "I was just trying to make a point."

"You understand, don't you Murph, that this is a very unusual situation we are dealing with here," Duncan said. "You wrote these messages on both a receipt and a piece of currency, and you used the same style of handwriting that Mr. Trowbridge used when he wrote the suicide note. And now Mr. Trowbridge is missing."

"Yes, I understand," I said.

I wondered if Duncan and Argyle could see right through me. In other words, did they get innocent people in their room all the time who were reduced to babbling idiots out of a fear of false imprisonment caused by viewing too much television? I was willing to bet they did. I was also willing to bet it was the guilty people who remained as cool as cucumbers, who acted suave and sophisticated, who casually puffed on cigarettes and blew smoke rings and smirked with derision at every question asked—people like James Cagney and Ernest T. Bass. No doubt Duncan and Argyle could separate the wheat from the chaff. For all I knew they were amused by my skittish alarm. That was all right with me, as long as they let me go home. I'm easy.

"I think we're finished with you for now, Murph," Duncan said. "We might need to call you in later to identify Mr. Trowbridge's body."

I nodded. I noted that he didn't say whether or not they actually had the body.

"Thanks for cooperating with us, Murph," Argyle said.

"You're welcome."

I waited for the cuffs to come out. But Duncan and Argyle merely stood up and told me that a patrolman would take me back to Rocky Cab. They said they were sorry that I had missed out on a couple hours of work. But I told them I didn't mind. This was true. I would be driving a taxi for the rest of my life, so a couple of hours didn't matter. Or did it? Have you ever tried to play catch-up on a late credit card payment? It's like rearranging treadmills on the *Titanic*.

I rode back to Rocky Cab in the rear of a patrol car. I recognized the cop, but he didn't seem to recognize me. Three years earlier he had knocked on my door and told me that he had found my stolen Chevy in an alley off Wewatta Street in LoDo. Wewatta Street was named after the wife of William McGaa, a mountain man who was one of the founders of Denver. Wewatta was a Lakota Sioux. In college I wrote a history paper on William McGaa because he is considered Denver's first official tosspot.

The cop was smart. He asked me if I wanted him to drop me off down the block from Rocky Cab. He thought I might be embarrassed to be seen getting out of a cop car where I worked. But I told him no. I said he could drop me at the front door. It would make me feel cool to climb out of a police car in front of everybody I knew. I always jump at opportunities to feel cool. But nobody was outside Rocky Cab when I climbed out. I felt like a fool.

When I got into the on-call room, I saw Stew seated inside the cage. This struck me as odd. Rollo is the day-man at Rocky Cab. I thought about asking Stew where Rollo was, then decided not to. I had fielded enough answers for one day. I just wanted to get back on the road and forget about everything. I wanted it to be a typical taxi Tuesday.

"Hogan wants to talk to you," Stew said, when he saw me come in.

I began to experience what I call "cabbie consciousness." This is a heightened state of awareness caused by an accumulation of experiences culminating in a brand of wisdom that you acquire after driving a taxi for ten years. It gives you the ability to size up situations in a millionth of a second. It's similar to my Univac, except that cabbie consciousness spits out the same message every time: "Trouble."

I nodded and said thanks. I figured Hogan would want to know the upshot, the lowdown, and the inside info on the missing-persons investigation. I was wrong.

"Have a seat," he said, as I entered his office.

That was the worst thing he could have said. Hogan never offers me a seat unless things are bad.

Real bad.

I sat down slowly and watched as Hogan removed his pop-bottle eyeglasses and cleaned them with a handkerchief and jammed them back on. Thank God I wear contacts.

"Murph … I didn't say anything about this yesterday, but you were in violation of regulations when you gave your fare, Mr. Trowbridge, that blank taxi receipt."

I nodded rather than spoke. Sometimes words can be just a little too … I don't know … I want to say "superfluous" but I think I mean "embarrassing."

"I was willing to let it go, Murph, because as far as I was concerned it was a trivial matter. But now that Mr. Trowbridge is missing, things are different. I had to report the incident to the owners of Rocky Cab, and I'm afraid I'm going to have to suspend you."

I gotta hand it to my cabbie consciousness. It's good. I sighed. I had been there before. The last time it happened though, the police never turned up a dead body. I didn't murder the eighteen-year-old girl to begin with.

"For how long?" I said.

Hogan reached up and began rubbing the back of his neck. "This is hard, Murph, but … the suspension is going to last until the police find the body of Mr. Trowbridge. After the investigation is over and they have determined the cause of the suicide ..."

"They think I had something to do with it," I said.

Hogan stopped talking. The one thing a cabbie never does is interrupt a supervisor when he's talking. The relationship between a cabbie and his supervisor is not informal. Cab driving is a risky business overseen by the Public Utilities Commission, and passenger safety is the number one priority of driving, and a driver who argues with a supervisor or shows the slightest contempt or disrespect for him or any other company personnel can count on losing his privilege to prowl the mean streets of Denver. And there I was, interrupting Hogan.

He stopped rubbing the back of his neck and looked at me. Then he went on talking as if I hadn't spoken. "After the investigation is over, your status will be reviewed by Mr. Hapworth." Hapworth owns RMTC.

"And the PUC, and the insurance company, and the mayor's nephew, right?" I said.

I was starting to freak, and I'll tell you why. I had been called on the carpet a lot of times in my life, and the more formal the boss acted, the more serious the consequences. I knew I was about to be fired from driving a taxi, and not just from Rocky Cab but from every company in Denver and maybe the entire United States of America, including the territories where the iron fists of the fruit companies keep the workers oppressed—like Oregon.

Hogan nodded.

"I'm sorry about this Murph. If you hadn't given Mr. Trowbridge that blank receipt, things might not have been so bad. But what with that, plus your cab burning up, plus Mr. Trowbridge's suicide, a determination was made."

"Am I being blamed for my cab burning up?" I said. I was aiming for a little umbrage here, but it was hollow umbrage. I had already blamed my cavalier attitude toward reality for the accident.

Hogan rubbed his chin. "Let me put it this way, Murph. As far as the insurance company was originally concerned, the case on your cab was closed. But then this Trowbridge business came up, so now they're looking into it again … along with the police."

"What do they expect to find?" I said.

Hogan shrugged. It was an honest shrug. I had never known Hogan to lie about anything. Of course we practically never spoke about anything at all, which skewed the matrix I suppose. "You'll have to turn in your key and trip-sheet to Stew," Hogan said.

"Where's Rollo?" I said.

Hogan sighed. He looked down at the desk, then looked up at me. "After you paid for your lease, Rollo noticed the strange writing on the bills, so he brought them up and suggested that you were defacing currency in violation of federal law. I recognized a sentence you had written on the receipt … the one about holding a job … so I figured the police had to see it. I told Rollo to run down to the dispatcher and give you an el-two while I called the police. When it looked like I was taking him seriously about the defacement, he asked if he could have the rest of the day off."

There was a moment of silence as unspoken words passed between Hogan and myself. Rollo had nailed my ass to the wall and had then bugged out. That made me feel good. I reigned in what little was left of the umbrage I had concocted out of thin air, and nodded.

"I understand," I said. "You're right. I shouldn't have handed out a blank receipt. My fault."

"I'm glad you see it that way, Murph."

"I've got an answering machine at home," I said. "If anything ever turns out okay, give me a call. I'll be around. I haven't had a real vacation in fourteen years anyway."

"I'll call you the minute I get the word," Hogan said. That was the end of that meeting.

I walked out and closed the door. I went downstairs and dug my key and trip-sheet out of my briefcase and handed it to Stew. Stew didn't know what was going on. I didn't explain. But he would find out. The Word gets around Rocky Cab at the same speed that The Word gets around every place where two or more human beings come together to be nosy. In this case though it was three words: Murph was out.

CHAPTER 22

I had been driving a taxi for fourteen years, longer than I had done anything in my life except watch TV. I thought about this as I drove my heap out of Rocky Cab and headed toward Capitol Hill. For the past fourteen years I had lived in a kind of hermetically sealed world, like one of those glass balls filled with water and artificial snow that billionaires drop off their deathbeds. It was a safe and secure little world where the past couldn't touch me and the future was only a rumor. I had lived hand-to-mouth and had been happy, because I was sustained by the belief that I would sell a novel someday and never have to worry about money again.

This belief actually had begun when I was a kid and didn't understand much about books. My Maw was reading *Peyton Place* one evening, so I asked her where the book had come from, and she explained that novels were written by people who got paid to write them. But I just meant where did she buy it, because a friend had told me it was a dirty book and I wanted to shoplift a copy of my own. But her explanation staggered me. They paid people to write books!!! Until that moment I had a vague idea that books were produced in factories, like tires, or else they grew on trees, like money.

I eventually got around to reading *Peyton Place,* and it wasn't pretty— I was on guard duty in the army that night so maybe I shouldn't delve too deeply into that, but the point is, I immediately realized I could write stuff like that, too. Maybe "realize" isn't the right word—"belief" or "delusion" or "who's kidding who" might best summarize my attitude.

But I never once doubted that it would happen, that I would become a bestselling author and never have to worry about money again.

I was only a kid.

And now here I was, forty-five years old and unemployed and still worrying about money. I don't know how many times during the previous fourteen years I had contemplated throwing in the towel and heading back to Wichita and asking my Maw to let me hole up in my old room long enough to figure out what to do with the rest of my life. Maybe it was *Psycho* that stopped me from going home. I've seen that movie more than any movie ever made—if you don't define TV shows as movies. For the purpose of incoherent self-reflection, I won't. Norman Bates never left home, and look what happened to him: he got to see Janet Leigh naked. If that had ever happened to me, I'd go bughouse, too.

I began to think that maybe it was time to find another line of work altogether. I guided my heap into the heart of Capitol Hill wondering for the first time in fourteen years what I could do to get money besides drive cabs or rob banks. Both occupations had their pros and cons. For instance, bank robbery isn't quite as dangerous as cab driving, but it pays better.

I knew where all this was headed. *The Denver Post.* I would be reading the classified ads in the morning. Not that I expected to find a job from the paper, since any job worth doing would have ten thousand applicants lined up at the warehouse door before I even woke up. But searching the classifieds for a job is sort of like practicing Transcendental Meditation. It preps you mentally for the scourge of "doing things."

I first began practicing CM (classified meditation) after I dropped out of college and was living in a boarding house in Cleveland. I needed a job. It was winter. It was cold. I was broke. I was unpublished. One day I was walking down the street when I saw a guy passing out handbills. It gave me an idea. I bought a newspaper. You can take it from there.

I climbed the fire escape to my crow's nest and entered my kitchen, wondering how many times I had done that. A minimum of once a day for fourteen years, minus trips to the liquor store. Then I tried to multiply three hundred and sixty-five times fourteen. By "tried" I mean I gave up after two seconds.

I didn't watch TV that night. I didn't cook a burger. I did drink a beer, and then another, and then another. Next thing I knew I had killed three beers. When I woke up the next morning I was still wearing my Keds. I knew it was time to either join AA or else not join and say I did. I decided instead to find a job.

I don't subscribe to the *Post,* but I don't subscribe to almost everything. Ergo, I had to walk down to the corner box and buy a paper. You heard me right. Buy. I know it's considered hip to wait for a businessman to purchase a newspaper from a box and then act like you intended to buy one at the exact same moment as he, so you reach for a paper while he's got the plastic lid open and you pretend to put a quarter in the slot as Mister Businessman opens his paper to the financial section while you make a lot of noise tapping the quarter against the edge of the box and hiding the coin-slot from his view and ...

Well—that's what hoodlums tell me anyway. But I believe in buying my papers. I don't know if I possess an inherent sense of morality or if I'm just chicken, and I don't want to know. I fed the box a quarter and walked home feeling obvious. I was certain that everybody I passed on the sidewalk knew I was unemployed and looking for work in the classifieds.

It felt good to be back in Cleveland.

When I got up to my crow's nest, I dropped the paper onto the kitchen table and took a moment to recall the proper method for practicing CM. It had been fourteen years, but it came back quickly because, unlike performing complex mathematical calculations, you never really lose your ability to look for a job. I popped open a beer, spread the classifieds on the table, then took a few minutes to read the front-page head-

lines, the comics, and the letters to the editor before I finally turned to …
wait a minute.

I froze.

I turned back to the front page. At the bottom right-hand corner was a small box with a headline: "Cab Driver Questioned In Missing Persons Case."

"A driver for the Rocky Mountain Taxicab Company, Brendan Aloysius Murphy, was questioned by police yesterday morning in reference to …"

Who the hell wrote this? How did he get my name? How did he even know I was brought down to DPD? What was going on here? For the first time in my life I found myself on the receiving end of The Written Word, a position traditionally held by shady politicians.

The story consisted of two short paragraphs, one convicting me of the kidnapping, robbery, and murder of a homeless man named Horace Trowbridge, and another paragraph completely exonerating me because the body of Mr. Trowbridge had not yet been found.

Yet.

I didn't know whether to wad the paper into a ball and throw it against the wall, or get a pair of scissors and cut the article out and paste it into my scrapbook next to my army discharge. That was one lonely scrapbook. I had always hoped something else would happen to me … but not this!

My first instinct was to get my copy of the Bill of Rights and reread the First Amendment. I wanted to double-check on the part that said anybody can write just anything.

My next instinct was to call the *Post* and demand to know the name of the so-called journalist who wrote this pseudo-trial transcript, and then go slug him in the guts.

I took a sip of beer to cool myself down. I started thinking about my travels around the country after I dropped out of WSU. I had lived for six months in Kansas City, where I used to enjoy reading the police blotter in a local rag. It was written by a reporter that called himself "Snoop" Jackson. He covered the police beat for the paper, as well as the emergency rooms of the various hospitals—the knife-and-gun clubs, etc. "Snoop" wrote a daily column called "Street Beat" and he covered the whole scene. KC was wide open when I lived there. It was kind of a focal point for what might be called the underground entertainment circuit. You could go to nightclubs and catch legendary black performers, jazzmen, bluesmen, and even white male college students. I used to devour it along with my hamburger breakfast. So who was I to complain that some local reporter was hot on my case? I decided not to slug anybody in the guts. Sure, I might become a hero to everybody in America, but from what little I knew about judges, they frowned on that sort of heroism. Actually I know quite a bit about judges, but let's not get into that.

I sighed with resignation. I decided the Founding Fathers undoubtedly knew their business when they wrote the First Amendment. Even back in 1776 there probably were hoodlums. I polished off my beer and started perusing the classifieds. Accountant. Bartender. Dancer. Engineer. Geologist. Hospital. Insurance. Landscape. Machinist. No Experience Necessary. That's what I was looking for. But after reading the ads I realized I didn't even qualify for that.

Then I started thinking about the day my Maw threw me out of the house. It had happened on the same day I announced that I was dropping out of college and marrying Mary Margaret Flaherty. Try as I might though, I could not recall the thread of logic that had led me to make those two "decisions," for lack of a better word. Mary Margaret refused to marry me, and my Maw refused to continue waiting on me hand-and-foot like a slave. So I left Wichita in a fit of pique determined to become a rich novelist. I ended up in Denver.

The End.

I continued to leaf through the classifieds until I came to Zoologist. What the heck would motivate a young person to become a zoologist? *Born Free*? I turned back to the A's and read the columns a little more closely. I originally had been hoping that my "Dream Job" would simply spring out at me as I speed-read the ads. I hate detail work.

During my first read-through I had intentionally skipped over the "Drivers Wanted" section for reasons that should be obvious to any nickel psychologist. But because the only thing I really knew how to do right was sit down, I decided to abandon my foolish pride and see if I could find a job that did not require a special license to operate a big-rig. The idea of long-haul truck driving had always appealed to me—the lure of the open road, the personal freedom—but I simply wasn't enough of a country music fan.

A number of ads said "Driver Needed" and gave a phone number. No hint as to what the job entailed. I was both intrigued and wary. Why wouldn't they describe the job? Were the bosses "up to something"? What if I called and they got annoyed at me? I skipped over those landmines and concentrated on the ads that had more than one line of text. I gritted my teeth when I saw an ad for the Rocky Mountain Taxicab Company. Hogan had written the ad, I could tell. "Cash Daily!!!" He knew his audience. Ernest Hemingway couldn't have said it shorter. Imagine William Faulkner writing help wanted ads.

Then it sprang out at me. "Flower Delivery." My heart began to race.

CHAPTER 23

I was sitting in the driver's seat of my flower delivery van outside a funeral home in east Denver. I was scared. How I had gotten there is not a long story, but I'm going to tell it to you anyway. I had applied for the delivery job at a shop called The Flower Pot on south Broadway and was hired on the spot, which rattled my nerves. The woman who hired me, Mrs. Carlysle, was a widower older than myself. She had a gorgeous and delightful nineteen-year-old daughter who did the flower arranging in the back room of the shop. The daughter does not appear again in this story.

My pay rate was three dollars per delivery, fifteen deliveries per shift, eight hours a day, five days a week. How's that for a mouthful of numbers? For you non-math majors out there, that adds up to $225.00 per week. I would be earning more money than I had ever made as a cab driver. I should have paid closer attention to the job market during the past forty-five years. But there were a number of drawbacks. For one thing, the nature of the job itself ran my ass ragged. Funeral homes were another drawback. Gone were the days of sitting outside a hotel at dawn, sipping a joe and savoring a Twinkie and reading a paperback book.

When I entered the flower shop at dawn on my first day of work, the floral arrangements were already set up on a table with addresses taped to the pots or fishbowls or ceramic cubes or whatever the customers had ordered. My job was to load them into the rear of the van, hop into the driver's seat, and hit the road running.

Believe it or not, I had to undergo training to do the job. Here is what my training consisted of: Mrs. Carlysle told me to be careful not to pick up a glass fishbowl by the rim, or a section of the glass would break off in my hand. She showed me how to reach under the bowl and lift it with the rounded bottom nestled in my palm. She had an anxious look in her eyes as she explained this procedure, so I figured the previous drivers had screwed up with regularity.

The fishbowls were usually fancy affairs, sort of like terrariums with a layer of colored sand on the bottom, and flowers sticking out the top. They could weigh up to five pounds. I told Mrs. Carlysle that I understood the procedure, which I did, but what's that got to do with my life? I just prayed I didn't forget to perform the procedure in the proper manner. I had recited the same prayer daily after what had come to be known as "The Incident" at the hand-grenade range in basic.

So there I was, seated inside my van outside a funeral home in east Denver trying to work up the courage to go inside. I had been told that the delivery entrance would be a door inside an open garage. It was my first funeral home. I was as nervous as a teenager on his first date. I'm a Baby Boomer, so I turned teen at the cusp of the era where dating was in remission and boys and girls simply started hanging out together without the bourgeois formalities of phone calls, boxes of candy, corsages, doorbells, berserk fathers, 3 A.M. calls to the police, stern lectures, and an innocent kiss goodnight. Kids today don't know what they're missing, thank God.

The floral arrangement scheduled for this drop-off had a type of flower called bird of paradise set in a wicker basket. I would learn that overall this seemed to be the preferred flower with which relatives honored their departed loved ones. When me ol' Dad died eight years ago, me Mither did our living room in shamrocks. But I didn't pay much attention to the decorations because I was in shock—my Maw wanted me to read a selection from *Finnegans Wake* during the eulogy. How I got through that sentence I'll never know. Can anybody tell me what "... the murk of the mythelated in the barrabelowther ..." means? None of my drunk uncles seemed to know.

I opened the door and climbed out of the van, went around to the rear and threw open the double doors. I picked up the wicker basket by the bottom. I was trying to develop a habit of picking up all the arrangements in this manner on the theory that I would get so used to it that I would accidentally pick up the fishbowls properly. I'm such a slave to habit that I had faith in this procedure. I won't keep you in suspense. It worked.

I carried the basket up the driveway and entered the garage, and came face-to-face with two doors. Mrs. Carlysle hadn't said anything about two doors. There were no signs to indicate which door to open. I didn't want to open the wrong door and walk in on a dead body. I chose the door to the left, opened it, and saw a dead body. It was lying on a clinic table with a towel draped across the waist. I backed away like a robo-coward, set the floral arrangement on the floor of the garage, and got the hell out of there.

Drawbacks, as I say. The job paid well, but I had the feeling that this was a mere taste of what I was in for if I made a career out of "blossom dissemination," which is the U.S. Department of Labor's title for what I was doing for a living. The turnover rate in the blossom dissemination racket is understandably high. I had very rarely encountered dead bodies as a cabbie.

As I sped away from the funeral home looking for a 7-11 and a cup of strong joe, I wondered if James Joyce had chosen the name Leopold "Bloom" in *Ulysses* for reasons which up until that moment had not occurred to me. I really should have stayed awake in college.

Without thinking, I pulled into the 7-11 at Quebec and Colfax. It was only when I parked and saw the on-duty clerk that I realized my blunder. The clerk was a former Rocky driver named Mickey. I jammed the van into reverse and pulled out, wheeling past the gas pumps and onto Colfax. I didn't want Mickey to see me. I was too embarrassed. We had known each other for ten years. He had quit Rocky Cab after he had gotten married, as do so many ex-bachelor hacks. It didn't occur to me that clerking a 7-11 might be analogous to flower delivery, two perfectly respectable jobs, and that the manner by which I earned my keep might mean less to Mickey than the life of a gnat. But try and tell that to my ego.

Okay. I'll admit it. I patronized a Starbucks that day. I was desperate for joe. I needed it bad. Real bad. Dead bodies are one thing, but when you add acute embarrassment to the mixture, sanity goes straight down the crapper. I carried a spray of begonias into the Starbucks and pretended I was lost and needed directions, and what the hell, as long as I'm here, give me a mocha.

My first day of work lasted only eight hours. I was used to twelve as a cabbie, so when it came time to go home I felt like I was playing hooky. It felt great. For one thing, the sun was still up, which gave me an extra four hours to sleep. Of course I was in "work shock." I had never held a job quite like this before, hauling flowers around town instead of a cargo of human flesh. And I didn't have to talk to anybody during the ride except the flowers. I could pour out my heart to them without incurring derision. I sang all the colorful songs I had written as a cabbie. I laughed whenever I passed a taxi on the street and yelled "Sucker!" Things were going so well that I became afraid. Who was I kidding? A job this good could never last. What was the catch? The catch of course resided in my heart. I was not a flower delivery man and I knew it. I was an asphalt warrior. It was that simple. I knew I was sitting in the wrong driver's seat. I felt like a scab. I also felt like reading paperbacks and nibbling Twinkies. I was driving eight hours a day non-stop, and as much as I loved it, I hated it. My only artistic accomplishment as a blossom disseminator was the composition of a song called "Born To Loaf," co-written by Ray Charles.

But this was my life now. I had no illusions about "the phone call" from Hogan. Work is a form of refuge "they" say, and they weren't getting an argument out of me. I threw myself into it. I drove on a Monday, a

Tuesday, and a Wednesday. After I got home Wednesday evening I made dinner, watched a Gilligan's, and channel-surfed for a bit. After it got dark outside I finally surrendered to my most uncontrollable vice and jotted down the amount of money that I calculated I had earned from the forty-five deliveries I had made so far. One hundred and thirty-five bucks. I felt like a first-time novelist calculating how much money he was going to make as soon as he heard from his publisher.

Since I was alone in my apartment and nobody could see me, I went ahead and added thirty more deliveries to my calculations just for fun. It was similar to typing "The End" on a blank sheet of paper when I was in college so I could see how it felt to finish writing a novel. It felt pretty good—two hundred and twenty-five bucks worth.

Then I started to daydream. This often happens when I think about money. As I was daydreaming, my eyes started roaming around the room. I know what you creative writing teachers are thinking: eyes can't roam. They don't have legs. Be precise blah blah blah. Anyway, I was thinking about how much money I would have if I added up two weeks worth of paychecks, when my eyes suddenly fell on my answering machine. I had eight messages. The red digit kept blinking 8, 8, 8, etc.

This annoyed me to the extent that the blinking was like somebody politely reminding me that I had an obligation I ought to fulfill, and there is nothing that annoys me more than a demand disguised as a gentle reminder—except losing my TV remote. I turn psycho.

I set my pencil aside and reached for the button to play the messages. Click. "Oh sorry, wrong number," someone said. Two of the messages consisted of hissing silences followed by rattling receivers. A woman said, "Bill?" Three messages were from telemarketers trying to sell me insurance or rug cleaner or something. Then the eighth message came on the machine and a familiar voice said, "Mister Murphy? My name is Horace Trowbridge. I just want you to know that I am not dead."

Click.

I froze.

I don't know how long I stared at the machine, but at some point I started to reach out to hit the replay button. I quickly pulled my hand back. I was afraid I might accidentally erase what could very well be the only piece of evidence that could save me from the chair, or the flower shop.

A half-dozen thoughts strafed my mind, such as, *What the hell is going on here?* and *I should call the police*—as well as the ever-popular, *Is my life in danger?* I had a few other thoughts in a similar vein, but these were uppermost, especially the one about "danger." Number two would be the thought about the "police." The "hell" thought goes through my mind every waking moment of my life, so it probably shouldn't even count.

I might have gone on staring and thinking forever, but then something strange occurred. My doorbell rang. I sat up straight and listened. The doorbell in my apartment has a muffled sound to it, caused by caked dust. Whenever my friends used to visit me, before I convinced them not to, they always came up the rear fire escape. They never used the front door. This indicated to me that a stranger must be at the front door. I felt ambivalent about this. In other words, which would I rather not be visited by—a friend or a stranger?

The second time the doorbell rang, I decided to treat it like a telephone bell. I simply waited for the caller to give up. Brother, if you think telephones are brutal, doorbells are the spawn of Satan.

The third ring was excruciating. Was this going to last forever? Then it occurred to me that it might be a cop, or else the IRS. Pavlov had me by the short hairs. I listened for the next ring, and found myself leaning forward in my chair like a man battling a hurricane-force wind. Then a chill went up my spine. I suddenly realized who was downstairs.

I went to the closet and pulled out my dusty baseball bat. I left my apartment by the hallway door and crept down the interior stairwell, which was carpeted, muffling the sound of my footsteps. I came to the ground floor and placed my ear against the front door and listened. I didn't hear anything.

I debated whether or not to say, "Who's there?" or just fling the door open. Either way I was a dead man. I wasn't kidding myself. I had seen enough Hitchcock to know Trowbridge was coming after me. These are the kinds of thoughts you have late at night in a black foyer. I do anyway. Then it occurred to me that if Trowbridge was out to get me, he wouldn't have phoned ahead. I really ought to stop renting movies.

I kept the bat hiked on my shoulder, ready to swing. I unlocked the front door and pulled it open an inch. Nobody there. I opened it all the way and looked around, then closed it and went back up to my apartment. I debated whether to call the police and ask them to come over, or to just chauffeur my answering machine down to DPD and let a trained expert replay the messages.

Then I became aware of a subtle vibration. I knew the vibration. Somebody was coming up the back fire escape.

The light was burning in my kitchen, and I knew I didn't have time to shut it off before my visitor made it to the top step. In the old days when my friends used to come over, I kept the kitchen light off. This gave me time to rise from my chair, slap the living room light off, and dash to my bedroom before they got to the door. But now I was trapped.

Knuckles rapped on the door.

I gazed at the kitchen light bulb with loathing in my heart, then crept toward the door with my baseball bat.

"Who's there?" I said.

CHAPTER 24

"It's me," the stupid bastard said.

"Who is me?" I said.

"Harold."

In fact, I had recognized his voice instantly. I only said "Who is me" to buy time, but he replied before I could devise a ploy to get rid of him.

I unbolted the door and opened it an inch. It was Harold all right. He was wearing his civilian clothes. Tennis shoes. Jacket. Baseball cap. He almost looked like a Rocky driver. Was he mocking me?

"I'm sorry," I said, shaking my head no. "Intrusions by appointment only."

"Sweeney asked me to drop by," he said.

That changed the paradigm. I opened the door and allowed Harold to enter my apartment for the first and last time in his life. I casually slipped my bat behind the door and leaned it against the wall. I don't like people to know the secret of my Maginot Line. Harold came in smiling big. I expected him to say "Top o' the evening to ye, lad," but he just said, "I guess your front doorbell doesn't work."

"It was disconnected years ago," I wished.

"Oh. I was out front for five minutes waiting for you to answer because I could see the lights on in your windows."

"Why did Sweeney ask you to come by?"

"He wanted me to give you a message."

Harold started patting his coat pockets like he was searching for matches. I waited patiently as his pantomime played itself out. He withdrew a newspaper clipping and held it up for me to see. I recognized it. *The Denver Post.* Page one. Cab Driver Questioned In Missing Persons Case.

"Sweeney posted this on the bulletin board down at the tavern," Harold said with a smile.

I smiled back. "Nice to know I still got a few friends left in this town."

"I don't think so," Harold said. "The reason he posted it was so everybody would know why you've been eighty-sixed permanently from Sweeney's Tavern."

"What!"

"Yeah," he chortled, and I suddenly realized why he had been smiling all along. He was bearing bad news. Because he was young and hadn't gotten used to that aspect of adulthood, he was dealing with it the only way he knew how—like an animal. Raw emotion. The smile of terror. The chortle of fear.

"Sweeney kept waiting for you to come down to the tavern so he could personally eighty-six you forever. But you haven't been around in awhile, so he gave me this and asked me to drop by tonight to tell you in person that you can't ever come back again."

"Why not?"

"Sweeney told me to tell you that he doesn't want any murderers patronizing his establishment."

"Hell, half of Sweeney's customers ..." I started to say, then stopped. I had momentarily forgotten that sarcasm was lost on Harold.

"I'm not a murderer," I said. "I didn't have anything to do with the Trowbridge case."

Harold raised the article and closed his eyes. "Sweeney warned me that you would try to use your wily ways to lure me into your confidence, and that I shouldn't listen to anything you say. He told me that after I delivered my message, I should get away from your apartment as fast as my feet could carry me."

"He said that?"

"Those very words."

"You tell Sweeney for me that as a fellow Irishman and an English major, I'm disappointed. He could have opted for a more succinct worn-out cliché."

"I'm not listening to you, Murph."

"Join the club."

Harold started folding the clipping. His demeanor had changed. I watched his face as he folded and refolded the clipping a number of times. It was a like a goddamn map. Then I realized Harold was sad.

Fer the luvva Christ, who was I to hold this kid in such contempt? He reminded me of a dumb kid I once knew, a wet-behind-the-ears draftee who got shipped off to the army with two left feet and a mop bucket to stuff them in. His name was Wardholtzer. He bunked next to me in basic.

"Aaah, don't feel bad, Harold," I said. "Thanks for delivering the message. I appreciate it. You saved me the embarrassment of getting another bum's-rush in public."

"I don't feel bad," he said.

"I see tears in your eyes, kid."

"I'm coming down with a cold."

"Oh."

He tucked the article into his coat pocket and smiled at me with the satisfaction of a pointless job well done.

"Harold, I want you to come into my living room and listen to something," I said.

"Sweeney warned me that you would try to lure me into your living room, Murph, and he told me not ..."

"This is important, Harold. I got a phone call from a man who claims he's Trowbridge."

I walked into the living room and turned around. Harold was now standing by the refrigerator—I want to say "uncertainly" but I hate adverbs. Nevertheless, that's how he was standing.

He stepped up to the doorway between the kitchen and the living room, and stopped. I reached down and touched the play button on the answering machine, and prayed I wasn't erasing anything.

After the message ended, I looked at Harold. "Did that sound like the guy that you sold beer to at nine in the morning?"

He nodded, then looked around my living room suspiciously. I became annoyed at the adverbs that seemed to trail Harold everywhere. Then I saw his eyes gazing directly at my bookshelf of rejected manuscripts. To distract him from asking a question I had asked myself a thousand times, I said, "I guess I'm going to have to call the police and ask them to try and trace the call."

"Why don't you just hit caller ID?" he said, frowning at the "bricks" of typing paper that held up the shelves.

"What do you mean?" I said.

"Just hit caller ID on your answering machine."

"What are you talking about, Harold, I don't understand what you mean, what are you saying?" I said shrilly. I was rattled. Harold was starting to talk like a normal person.

He finally tore his eyes away from my monument to ineptitude and crossed the floor to the answering machine.

"Wow, an AudioMaster DeLuxe," he said, gazing admiringly at the machine. "You must have laid out some big bucks for this, Murph. I always took you for a cheapskate. How much did it cost?"

"I don't know. It was a gift."

"From who? A rich man ha ha."

"Yes. Now what's all this about caller ID?"

He pointed at a button that was clearly labeled Caller ID. "Haven't you ever pushed this button before?" he said.

"No. I only hit the play and erase buttons."

"What about these buttons?" he said, pointing at the thousands of buttons I had never even looked at, much less touched.

I grabbed his wrist. "Caller ID," I said. "What does that mean?"

He reached down and pressed the Caller ID button. I was still holding onto his wrist. It was horrible. I let go.

"See this little window?" he said, pointing at a small rectangular transparent plastic window that was backlit. A group of numbers appeared. "That's the phone number of the telephone that he called from."

"Really?"

"Yes. He called from the YMCA."

"What?" I said, frowning at the window. "How do you know? Does it say that on there somewhere?"

"Well ... as you know I'm a runner."

"No, I didn't know that," I lied.

"Really? I thought everybody knew I was a runner."

"I doubt if everybody knows anything about you, Harold."

"Each evening after work I go to the 'Y' and run laps on the indoor track," he said. "I sometimes call my girlfriend from there, and this is the telephone number of the pay phone at the 'Y.'"

"You have a gir ...?" I started to say, then I stopped. I tried to focus.

"That reminds me," Harold said, making me lose focus. "There's a couple of things I don't understand about this situation."

"Like what?"

"Did you give those two detectives my name?" he said. I froze.

I looked toward my baseball bat. "They forced it out of me," I said.

"That's what I thought," he said. "They came around last Monday and asked me questions about Mr. Trowbridge. They didn't tell me much about their investigation, but they wanted to know things about you.

They asked me about that funny five-dollar bill you showed me at the bar when those two ladies ...”

"Yeah, yeah, what about the five?"

"The policemen wanted to know where it came from, just like you did, except I got the feeling they thought you had written those words on it."

"What did you tell them?"

"I said I didn't know for sure."

"You said 'for sure'?"

"Yes."

"Oh Harold ..." I said, then I gave up, just like I gave up on Ward-holtzer.

"The detectives didn't tell me much, so I didn't really find out what it was all about until Sweeney posted this article." Harold started patting his pockets again. I grabbed his wrists and physically stopped his hands from moving.

"I hear you," I said, employing a cliché I loathe. "It's time for you to go."

I sounded just like one of my friends at a party. Where were my friends now, by the way? Surely the people I was closest to in Denver had read the article. Why hadn't I heard from any of them? The answer is contained in sentence number three.

"If you're coming down with a cold you ought to go right home and get to bed," I said, escorting him to the door. "You don't look so good."

"Really?"

"Yes. And try to refrain from running laps until hell freezes over."

"I knew I shouldn't have gone to the 'Y' this week, but I'm addicted to running."

"Vanilla isn't the only flavor of ice cream," I said. "There are other meaningless ways to kill time."

"I suppose."

"Take care of yourself, laddie," I said, as I opened the door.

He touched the bill of his cap as he walked out. "Top o' the evening to …"

I shut the door and bolted it. That bastard!

Trowbridge, I meant. What in the hell was going on here? I went to the living room and stared at the blank screen of my TV. It was like looking at my brain. I began to see images. They were like "thoughts." I could see myself driving down to the "Y" and bursting in. I immediately edited out the "bursting" part. I've been to the "Y" and it's run by jocks. Then I had another "thought." The YMCA information had come from Harold. Was it reliable? Harold wasn't a liar, but he was a twit, which can be worse. But Harold had graduated from a bartending school, so he wasn't a complete twit—he was the spiritual equivalent of a cabbie. I accepted the fact that I had to go to the "Y" and find out whether Harold had been mistaken or whether I had been used as a pawn in an inexplicable ruse of morally reprehensible proportions.

I glanced at my wristwatch. 7:30.

Then I had another "thought." I should get Duncan and Argyle on the phone and send them over to the "Y." But again—what if Harold was wrong? Goddamn that Harold. What if Duncan and Argyle found themselves on a wild-goose chase? And consider this—what if Trowbridge's body already had been found on the mountain? How would that make me look? Suspicious? Trying too hard to prove my innocence? But I am innocent, I insisted. Forget the missing man, the forged handwriting, the burning cab, I've never been implicated in a murder in my life except for that situation involving the eighteen-year-old girl, which I hope I have made clear to you was a completely ridiculous misunderstanding.

I started pacing the room as these "thoughts" strafed my mind. Bad move. I decided to sit down in my easy chair in order to think more clearly. It's not that I can't walk and think at the same time, but I have no other explanation.

I calmed down and focused again on my TV screen. I remembered a show I once saw where two men were trying to decide how to approach the solution to a problem, and one of them said, "Let's just assume that X is true, and then proceed from there." I was so impressed by that logic that I promised myself that I would someday write it down.

"If Trowbridge is at the YMCA right at this moment …" I mumbled.

I looked at my answering machine. I reached over and touched the button and replayed the message. "Mister Murphy? My name is Horace Trowbridge. I just want you to know that I am not dead."

Maybe I should just go ahead and call the police, I told myself. Maybe they could trace it and confirm what Harold had said. But what if Trowbridge had already left the "Y" and was scuttling down alleys? Time was of the essence. I had to move fast.

I got up and went to the bookshelf and withdrew my copy of *Finnegans Wake.*

Stale taxi profits were moldering in my Joyce. It was money that I had earned on my last day of driving. I hadn't touched any of it since I had begun delivering flowers. It was my intention to never touch it again as long as I lived.

Let me explain.

I sometimes see myself as a character in a movie about either my own or somebody else's life. It's a holdover from my childhood, similar to putting a towel over the bathroom mirror, which I quit doing after I was drafted. I had seen *High Noon* when I was ten, so I developed a habit of walking down the middle of our street in Wichita, somberly looking left and right like Gary Cooper. I was looking for gunslingers. I was certain that everyone in the neighborhood was watching me from their windows like a movie audience. I was right about that, but the point is, I sometimes make melodramatic Hollywood-style vows. But they are harmless vows, which is why I break them so often. Thus, the notion that I would never again touch the money hidden in my book was ludicrous, but it made me feel good to pretend it was true, and feeling good is the bottom line in my book.

I pulled out five of the five-dollar bills and put the book back on the shelf. I went to my briefcase and pulled out a ballpoint pen, then went to my combination writing/beer table and sat down. Slowly, carefully, and methodically, which is how I do practically nothing, I began to write sentences on the money.

CHAPTER 25

I went to my closet and yanked open the door. My deep forest green Rocky cap and jacket were draped on a hanger where they had been gathering dust since my last day of professional cab driving. I pulled them out of the closet, put on my jacket, and zipped it up. I carried my cap into the bathroom and stood in front of the mirror. I ran my fingers through my hair until my ponytail was hanging in accordance with strict barber regulations, then I placed the cap on top of my head and made sure it was squared away. I hadn't paid this much attention to the proper placement of clothing since the day I received my army discharge.

It felt good to be back in uniform. I was "going in."

I closed up my crow's nest, climbed down the back fire escape, and got into my heap. I sat there for one moment in the darkness of my car wishing I was in Rocky Mountain Taxicab #127. But that was long ago and in another parking lot, and anyway the hack was dead. And I knew who had killed it. I had known all along, I just wouldn't admit it to myself. Trowbridge had killed 127. Trowbridge with his trip down memory lane. Trowbridge with his nostalgic tales of youth. Trowbridge with his insistence that I drive him up a mountain road that proved too much for the taxi. Maybe a twelve-year-old boy had what it took to pedal five miles up a mock Matterhorn, but what does an aging auto know about scenic lookouts, soda pop, and stragglers? You put the eight-cylinder brute to work and pray to God the radiator cap doesn't blow a gasket and the brakes don't fade on the downhill run—and all your taxi asks in return is a chance to jump one more bell, and rest its weary axles outside one last hotel.

"Mr. Trowbridge—he dead," I said to the darkness. Then I started the engine.

I drove out of the parking lot and made my way to 13th Avenue. I pointed my hood ornament west toward that conglomeration of crooked streets known as "downtown Denver." The city was pretty that night. The sky was cloudless and black, the stars low and hard and white above the glow of windows running the length of the financial district, bright panes of glass in office buildings where janitors plied their lonely trade, windows in hotels, bars, cafés, and even 7-11 stores where men like myself were stopping in for a cup of hot joe and a quiet chat with a friendly ex-hack who had traded his cab license for a green apron and a wedding ring. I was of them, but I was not among them, because somewhere in the heart of Denver lived a man with the soul of a thief who had stolen the best of all possible jobs: Trowbridge. I would find the bastard before this night was through.

I cruised down the slope of The Hill on 13th, then turned right onto Lincoln Street. The YMCA was located between 17th and 18th. It still is. It's an old building, maybe nineteenth century, the kind of edifice that either wins or loses the race between the historic preservationists and the real-estate developers. I had seen plenty of those races since I first blew into town. I had seen both sides win a few and lose a few. It could get ugly. But I'd given up hope long ago that the races would be outlawed by an enlightened legislature that wanted to see the infrastructure of historic Denver rot with dignity. It's a story as old as Adam and Eve: nothing can stop progress, not even a mill levy and a prayer.

The "Y" was my starting point. I was going to assume that Trowbridge was there, and proceed from that assumption. If—and when—it proved a fruitless ploy, I intended to scour the streets in an ever-widening spiral, hitting the bowery bars and flophouses in search of a man who didn't stay long in one hideout. Due to the urban-renewal programs that had begun in the late 1960s, there weren't that many flophouses left in downtown Denver, which made my job a lot easier. Thank God for real-estate developers.

I parked at a meter along Lincoln Street right across the street from the "Y." It was after hours so the parking was free, but that didn't alleviate the sour feeling that boiled up in my gut—imagine a cabbie using a parking meter. But there weren't any cabbies on Lincoln Street that night. There was only me: a blossom disseminator waiting for the results of a suspension hearing already rigged by the hand of Fate. If Trowbridge really was dead, so was my dream of regaining my status as an asphalt warrior.

I jaywalked across Lincoln Street. It gave me the same thrill I used to get when I parked in no-parking zones, and I needed that thrill. I needed it bad. I needed to feel like an asphalt warrior again because I was about to enter the dragon's lair, which is located right across the street from the Knickerbocker Building.

I walked into the YMCA foyer and approached the main desk. The place was quiet. It was after 8:00 P.M. A man was seated behind the desk reading a newspaper. He was wearing a gray T-shirt, gym shorts, and tennis shoes. I pegged him as a jock.

"May I help you, sir?" he said, looking up from his paper. "Rocky Cab," I lied, pinching the bill of my cap. "I got a call on my radio to pick up a Mr. Trowbridge. The dispatcher told me he would be waiting outside but he isn't there. I wonder if you happen to know where he is."

The jock closed the paper and nodded. "Sure. He's got a room down the hall. You can knock and see if he's in."

As you might surmise, by the time the man had ceased speaking I was in shock. I leaned against the front desk to maintain my equilibrium. "How long has Mr. Trowbridge been living here at the 'Y'?"

"He took a room this morning."

I opened my mouth to ask a hundred questions, then remembered I was talking to a desk clerk. Desk clerks are like bartenders and cabbies.

You don't want to cross the line with a lot of questions. The operative word is "lot." A couple of questions are fine, as long as they possess a taint of "relevance." But when you start asking a lot of questions, the bloom goes off the rose and answers don't come so easy anymore. There's that word "bloom" again.

"He's in the last room at the end of the hall," the man said. "Please knock softly."

"Thanks, pal," I replied, feigning composure. I walked down the hall feeling like Gary Cooper on a particularly bad day.

I somberly glanced left and right as I made my way along the silent corridor. I came to the last room. I stood for a moment listening. This is an old cabbie habit—and like old cabbies, old habits die hard. I glanced back at the desk clerk. His nose was planted in the world of wars and sports and editorial cartoons. I knocked softly.

I listened closely. I didn't hear anything, so I tapped into my cabbie consciousness, but it reacted like a Geiger counter scouring an unpromising desert—Oppenheimer would have to look elsewhere for simple solutions to geopolitical quandaries.

But then …"Yes?" a voice said.

I had the feeling I had awakened someone from a sleep so deep that not even my cabbie consciousness could penetrate his dreams. Waking him up made me feel bad, but not too bad.

"Rocky Cab," I said.

I heard the standard fumbling sounds of a man grabbing fabric. I knew Trowbridge was pulling on his pants. All pants sound alike. Believe me, I've been there.

I heard the slippery sound of unshod feet approaching the other side of the door. "I didn't call a taxi," he said.

"Yes you did," I said. "You called a taxi for an unfinished ride to the top of Lookout Mountain."

Silence.

The knob rotated. The door opened a few inches. Trowbridge was wearing an undershirt and the same Bozo trousers that had followed me from Capitol Hill to Glenarm. He looked me up and down, and said, "What do you mean by that?"

"The police found your credit cards, Mr. Trowbridge," I said. "They found your wristwatch and your suicide note. And now I found you, and unless you let me in, I'm going to holler at the desk clerk to call the police."

He closed his eyes. When you've driven a cab as long as I have, you see a lot of closed eyes. I know my closed eyes. His read "resignation." He pulled the door open and nodded at me.

I stepped inside and looked around fast. Bed. Chest of drawers. Naked bulb overhead. I saw nothing to indicate that a man was living in this room, except the man himself.

I waited for him to ask me who I was, but he didn't. He shuffled back to his bed and sat down with a look on his face that indicated it didn't really matter who I was. Maybe his face had a point.

"I'm the Rocky Cab driver who took you from The Curtis Street Arms to the Blake Street Apartments," I said. "And from the Blake Street Apartments to a scenic point halfway up Lookout Mountain. I'm the driver who let you out at Glenarm and Broadway and watched you walk all the way to the men's mission."

As I spoke he raised his chin and looked at my face. I detected no recognition.

"I know," he said.

A chill ran up my spine. "What do you mean?" I said. "How do you know me?"

"I recognize you," he said.

"What do you mean—recognize me from where?"

"You're the driver who showed up each time I called a taxi last week. I recognized you then, too."

"Well if you recognized me, why didn't you say something like, for instance, 'Hello again, driver'?"

He shrugged. "I was embarrassed."

I decided to let that one go and get this conversation back on track. "You and me have a couple of things to discuss, Mr. Trowbridge."

He didn't nod, didn't shake his head no. He just waited. "I want to start with this," I said.

I reached into my shirt pocket and withdrew the five-dollar bills. On each bill was a string of words that looked like cartoon punch lines coming out of Abraham Lincoln's mouth. I had printed them for the same reason I had printed "You must not hold a job that you like" on a receipt that I had given to Trowbridge a week earlier, a reason I was not quite able to make clear to Duncan and Argyle. "Just messing around," I had told them. As good a reason as any, and better than most. Maybe it was the truth. Maybe messing around was all I had been doing after Trowbridge and I came down from the mountain and I slipped him a blank receipt. Maybe I was just curious, maybe I just wanted to get his reaction, wanted to find out what those messages were all about, and why he kept writing them down on five-dollar bills. But I wasn't messing around now. My life had undergone one too many big changes. My name had been removed from the roster of asphalt warriors. No. I wasn't messing around anymore.

I held the bills out to Trowbridge and said, "Can you tell me what these words mean?"

He looked up at me with eyes that said he really wasn't interested in what I had to show him. So I gave the bills a little shake, a physical indicator telegraphing a message that said neither of us would be leaving this room until he responded to my question. He took the bills and held them at an angle to catch the light from the bulb overhead. He began leafing through them. Something resembling a smile formed on his lips.

"Ah yes," he said. "These are the rules of The Heart of Darkness Club."

CHAPTER 26

Trowbridge looked up at me. "It's curious that you have these," he said. "Where did you get them?"

"Don't kid me," I said. "You know where I got them."

I was trying to call a bluff that I wasn't sure of. But then, isn't that the nature of bluffs?

"Wait a minute," he said. He frowned as he examined one bill in particular. "I've never seen this one before."

He raised the bill toward me. I didn't touch it, but I did recognize the handwriting. It was mine. So was the message. "You must not hold a job that you like."

"You don't recognize it because I wrote that one," I said. "You wrote the others."

Then he did something odd. He began nodding his head yes, then shaking it no. "I did conceive of these sentences"—yes—"but I didn't write any of these sentences"—no. "This isn't my handwriting."

He held the stack out to me like a man returning a favor. I snatched the bills and tossed them to the floor. "Okay Mr. Trowbridge, it's time to stop playing games. You're right, that isn't your handwriting. It's mine. I wrote those sentences on those fivers. I did it because I wanted to see the look on your face when you saw them, only your face disappointed me. It didn't tell me what I wanted to hear. So now I want your mouth to start talking. I want to know why you wrote those … rules … on the five-dollar bills you gave to me last week. I want to know why you gave one of those bills to a bartender at Sweeney's Tavern. I want to know why you threw your credits cards and wristwatch off Lookout Mountain. You may not know this, Mr. Trowbridge, but you cost me my job. The police think I murdered you. So I have one more question to ask before you start giving me answers: If I killed you, then why aren't you dead?"

He stared at me as I rattled off this litany of questions, then he lowered his head and softly said, "I had no intention of involving you in this business."

"What business?"

"My suicide."

A new breed of chill crept up my spine. Suddenly I wondered if I had stepped onstage just in time. I took another quick look around the room. I was searching for a straight razor, a noose, a gas range, anything that might be used by a man who was bent on going to hell the hard way. The room read empty. But for all I knew there was a pistol under his pillow, a bottle of pills in the chest of drawers, a box of rat poison under the bed.

"Are you planning to kill yourself?" I said. He shook his head no.

"Then why did you say that?" I said. He raised his head and looked at me.

"For the past few weeks I have been laboring under the assumption that if people thought I was dead, they would stop annoying me and leave me alone."

I didn't respond right away. I examined his statement from every angle, and while I admired the logic, the cockeyed optimism left me cold. If a man isn't dead, people are bound to find out, and after they do, they'll start annoying him. That could damn near be a … rule.

"What did you mean when you said these things were rules?" I said, stooping down and picking up the scattered money. I felt badly about littering a man's living quarters—my Maw didn't raise a savage in spite of what she might tell you—but there was more to it than that. In my estimation, I was in the presence of a man teetering on the brink of insanity, so I didn't want to annoy him. Fortunately I was a cab driver, so I wasn't completely in the dark.

"These are The Heart of Darkness Club rules," Trowbridge said, and a lilt of something resembling joy entered his voice. He smiled as I stood erect, stacking the bills together. "When I was a young man I was a member of The Heart of Darkness Club," he said. "What you hold in your hands are some of the rules. Not all … but some."

"What's The Heart of Darkness Club?" I said.

"That's difficult to say," Trowbridge replied. "The parameters of the club were never fully defined, but for the most part it consisted of a group of college boys who did their best to articulate their attitudes toward the meaninglessness of existence."

I froze.

"We also drank a lot of beer," he said. I started to thaw.

"It has been more than forty years since I belonged to the club—not that I ever ceased to be a member. That's another rule of The Heart of Darkness Club. You can never cease to be a member."

He raised his chin and began gazing at the far wall. He smiled. "Most of the rules of The Heart of Darkness Club were never written down. In fact, trying to nail down all the rules of The Heart of Darkness Club was a risky proposition, because it could jeopardize your membership in the club."

"Why is that?" I said.

"Because it reeked of ambition."

I started to ask how your membership could be jeopardized if you could never cease to be a member, but I stopped myself. I was dealing with a concept invented by drunk college boys.

"If you ask me, it sounds like a fraternity of louts," I said. He raised his eyebrows, then asked if I had a pen.

"Why?" I said.

"I would like to write that down."

I raised the bills. "The way you wrote these down?"

"Yes," he said.

"You still haven't answered my question. Why did you write these sentences on the bills?"

"Because they were handy."

"What do you mean?"

"The bills were the only pieces of paper I had at the time."

"I don't think we're on the same page," I said, utilizing another revolting cliché. "I want to know why you go around writing messages on five-dollar bills. What was your motive, your rationale, your inciting incident?"

He squinted at me. "You're an English major, aren't you?" he said, but it wasn't really a question. It was an indictment.

"That's irrelevant," I said. "I want some answers."

"All right," he said. "It has been forty years since I was a member of the club, and during the past week or so I have been trying to recall the exact wording of as many of The Heart of Darkness Club rules as possible. When you knocked on my door this evening I was trying to work out the wording of the longest rule." He reached under the pillow.

I grabbed my squeeze bottle.

Did I mention that I was armed when I entered his room that night? Sometimes I pack a nasal-spray bottle filled with ammonia if it looks like I might be toying with danger. In fact, carrying a squirt bottle filled with ammonia can be dangerous in and of itself, so you have to stay on your toes. It's best to leave your weapon at home during the flu season, as well I know.

But instead of pulling out a loaded gat, Trowbridge pulled out a sheet of paper, and it wasn't manufactured at the Denver mint. Come to think of it, they only make coins at the Denver mint. Nevertheless, it wasn't a greenback, it was a sheet of typing paper. I holstered my plastic bottle.

He held the paper out to me, but I shook my head no. "Not interested," I said, then I sorted through the bills until I found the one I was looking for. I held it up. "When I was driving you back from Lookout Mountain, did you write this sentence?" I read it aloud: "'You must be compelled by an inner force to read books, listen to music, and view films which serve only to send you spiraling deeper into the bottomless pit of frustration.'"

He nodded. "It was on the downward journey that I recalled the exact wording, syntax, and grammar."

"Why did you write it on the bill?"

"As I said, it was handy. I had a pocket full of bills."

"But after you wrote it down, why didn't you hold onto it?"

"No need. Once I had it written down, it became locked in here," and he tapped his skull.

"So this wasn't some sort of secret message intended to be read by me?"

"Heavens no. I intended to make it a part of my suicide note, and I wanted to get it right."

"What in the hell kind of suicide note were you writing?"

"A fairly melodramatic one, I suppose."

"But why would you do that if you weren't really going to kill yourself?"

"So people would leave me alone."

"What people?"

He clasped his hands on his lap and gazed at the far wall. "My ex-wife. Her family. My family. My neighbors. The Internal Revenue Service. My business associates. My …"

"Alright, alright, I get the picture," I said.

I did, too. Did I ever mention the fact that I have never met any of the other tenants who live in my apartment building? And I've lived there for sixteen years. "Okay, you want to be left alone," I said. "Who doesn't?

But faking a suicide? Don't you know there are laws against pretending not to exist?"

"Yes, I do."

"The minister who runs the men's mission called the police, and the police interrogated me," I said. "They think I pushed you off Lookout Mountain."

Trowbridge bowed his head. "I know. I read about it in the paper."

"Is that where you learned my name? Is that how you managed to track down my phone number and leave me a message that meant everything and nothing to me?"

"Yes."

"How in the hell did you get my goddamn phone number anyway?"

"The phone book."

"Oh."

I had forgotten about the only book I hate more than *Peyton Place*. No wonder I get crap messages on my answering machine day and night.

Trowbridge looked up at me. "The article mentioned you. That's when I realized I had inadvertently involved you in this ... this ill-planned scheme. That's why I left that message on your answering machine. I wanted you to know that I was in fact alive, and that the authorities would not be able to charge you with murder."

I frowned. "I've never known a missing corpse to stop a determined DA from charging anybody with anything," I said, which was true. "What the hell was your plan anyway?"

Trowbridge sighed. He looked up at me. "I intended to get rid of all my belongings a piece at a time, moving from here to there, leaving a kind of trail that I hoped would cause everybody to believe that I intended to take my life. By the time I disappeared I hoped that they would be convinced."

"You tossed your credit cards and wristwatch off Lookout Mountain, didn't you?"

"Yes."

"You did it surreptitiously while we were up there, didn't you?"

"Yes."

"You never intended to go all the way to Buffalo Bill's grave, did you?"

"No."

"Which means you did intend to involve me in your fake suicide."

He opened his mouth and said, "I didn't intend…" but he didn't finish.

So I finished it for him. "You didn't intend for me to get charged with murder, all you wanted was a witness who would lead the police to those bits of evidence you tossed away. Am I right?"

He nodded.

"Well … it worked," I said. "But I got lucky. The police let me off the hook. But they're still looking for your body on the side of Lookout Mountain."

Trowbridge sat perfectly still and didn't respond. He sat so motionless that I experienced something like déjà vu, only different. He reminded me of myself on the day I sat in the small room at DPD trying to look innocent, the hardest act to pull off when you're not guilty. I suddenly realized that his ex-wife, family, IRS, and everybody else on his list weren't the only people he wished would leave him alone. I was on that list, too. Frankly, I'm on a lot of those lists, but let's not get into that. I will say this though: Trowbridge and I could have traded lists and they would have been damn near identical, the only difference being that I had never gotten around to acquiring an ex-wife—and I even knew who she wasn't: Mary Margaret Flaherty of Wichita, Kansas.

"If you wanted to disappear," I said, "why didn't you just leave the country? South America is said to be far away at this time of year."

"I prefer to live in North America," he said.

"I hear you," I said, and this time it didn't bother me to say it. I really like North America.

I took a step backward, which wasn't easy to do in that small room, but I did it to give Trowbridge the sense that I didn't want to crowd him.

"Listen, Mr. Trowbridge, it's none of my business how you want to live your life or fake your death, but after the big boys down at Rocky Cab found out the police were asking questions about you and me, they pulled my license. Right now I'm delivering flowers for a living, and I want to get back to my real vocation. But if you pull a disappearing act, it means I'm out for good, and that's where I draw the line. I can't let you do it. I'm going to call the police and tell them you're here. I'm sorry if that tosses a monkey wrench into your plan because, to be honest, I like your plan. There've been plenty of times when I wished I could drop out of sight, or drop out of society, or at least sink through the floor. I'm sure if every man looked hard enough, he could remember a moment in his life when he wished he could have slipped out the back door when nobody was looking. The maternity ward comes to mind. But I can't let you disappear, Mr. Trowbridge. You're the last living link to my meal ticket."

At some point during this soliloquy, Trowbridge had begun nodding his head. This made me feel bad. I always feel bad when people agree with me. I start losing respect for their I.Q.

He folded the sheet of paper that he had been holding. It was a gesture of finality. He looked up at me and said, "I'm ready to face the music."

His statement was like a hatchet in my heart. This man was headed for jail and I knew it. But who was I to put anybody in jail? There were at least two men in the room who deserved to be jailed that night, but let's not delve very deeply into that, although I'm not talking legal technicality so much as moral imperative—my friend Big Al could bend your ear on that subject to the tune of $1.50 per mile.

But what could I do? Remain a blossom disseminator for the rest of my life? Or even worse, get a job? Sure, I could have let Trowbridge go. I could have pretended I had never found him holed up in a corner room at the "Y," licking wounds inflicted on him by a life too cruel to endure. I could have faked it. I'm good at that. I'm a pro. But what was one man's salvation compared to my personal comfort? That was the dilemma I pretended to wrestle with as I escorted Mr. Trowbridge down the hall to the front desk.

When I asked the jock if I could use the telephone at the front desk, he told me I would have to use the pay phone next to the Coke machine. So I told him that this was a police matter involving a murder/suicide. That rattled his dumbbells and saved me a quarter. He placed the call himself on the official "Y" phone.

Jocks.

Give me a break.

CHAPTER 27

Does this story have a happy ending? That depends on your definition of "ending." But I won't keep you in suspense—that's Mickey Spillane's job. Trowbridge was required by a judge to take a little "vacation" in the same sort of hermetically sealed glass ball where Norman Bates whiled away his life until the script for *Psycho II* was greenlighted. I'll admit it. I've seen all IV of the Psycho movies. I'm easy. Anthony Perkins himself directed #III, for those of you looking for an excuse to wander down to the video store later. But as both an English major and a film buff, I caught myself comparing and contrasting the Hitchcock version with the sequels, and I came to the conclusion that it's best to stick with a fraud who knows what he's doing. By "fraud" I am referring to someone who has thoroughly mastered the illusion of motion—something I mastered in Phys-Ed, i.e., every time my gym coach looked at me, I appeared to be coming down from the climbing rope. Alfred Hitchcock was the best teacher I ever had.

I never saw Mr. Trowbridge again. When the police showed up at the YMCA, I explained the situation to them, and made a special point of name-dropping Duncan and Argyle, which cut through the red tape. The patrolmen whisked him away. Strangely, I didn't recognize either of the officers who escorted him to DPD. Between my two-toned heap and the stolen car racket, I had assumed I had met every cop on the Denver police force. But I found out later that there are more than four thousand of our finest working the street beat, so it'll take another year or two before I meet them all.

As I watched the patrol car pull away from the curb that night, I knew in my heart that I wasn't going to try to keep track of the disposition of the Trowbridge Case. Did that make me a bad person? You be the judge. I was too busy feeling guilty. But I also knew I would find out sooner or later because there was still the matter of my suspension hearing. At some point the big boys at Rocky would learn the outcome of the suicide investigation and make a decision about me. Just for kicks though, I think I'll keep you in suspense.

I drove back to my crow's nest that night with the bitter taste of victory in my mouth. It's a funny thing about victory—its effects never last as long as defeat. Back in the days when I suffered from the delusion that I knew how to bet on the dogs, a win was such an aberration that the joy lasted about as long as a photo-finish—one thousandth of a second. Then it was back to the tip-sheet and the ticket window and the delusion that I knew how to bet. My friend Big Al eventually held an intervention and cured me of going to the track. He also expressed an interest in curing me of mailing manuscripts to publishers, but I suggested he enter a rehab program for people addicted to playing God. Things are currently at a standoff.

I intended to go to work at The Flower Pot on Thursday morning. My innocence had already been established in the Trowbridge Case, as far as the police were concerned. They had him in custody. Yet there I was, still disseminating blossoms and waiting for The Word. I felt like a character in a Kafka novel waiting for the machineries of bureaucracy to get in synch with reality. Anthony Perkins starred in the movie version of Franz Kafka's novel, *The Trial*. It was directed by Orson Welles. I personally find it unwatchable, but Leonard Maltin gives it three and a half stars. I sometimes think Orson Welles was too ambitious for his own good, not counting *Casino Royale*.

"The phone call" came when I wasn't at home. I found it on my answering machine. Hogan told me to make it down to Rocky Cab on

Friday if I was available, because we had something to talk about. This is another one of the many reasons I hate telephones: the partial newsflash. Hey, if you've got something to say, say it. I sometimes get messages from people who say, "It's me, give me a call, it's important." Who the hell is me? I've asked myself that question a thousand times.

But I have a theory that people think the telephone gives their minds legitimacy. I'm talking the generic fallacy here—i.e., if it's printed in the newspaper, it must be true. In Ma Bell's case, if someone leaves you a phone message, it has to be as serious as a court order. I was at a Bronco pre-game party once in a friend's backyard, and his phone started ringing. His wife nearly broke her ankles racing into the house. What the hell is it about a telephone that fills people with the fear of God? But I think I know the answer. When a phone rings, everybody in America thinks the lottery is calling. Me included. After all, I do listen closely to those messages.

On Friday morning I went to work at The Flower Pot with a sense of trepidation that I had not felt since the last time I'd walked off a job, which was Dyna-Plex. There's something about quitting jobs that fills people with the fear of God, too, and I think I know what it is: you're afraid your boss won't like you anymore.

I told Mrs. Carlysle that this was my last day, then I waited for her to get annoyed with me. She was filling a wicker basket with bird of paradise blooms. But she just smiled and went on arranging the flowers. I knew then that she was a pro. You don't make it in the blossom dissemination racket by having faith in truck drivers. She asked me what I was going to do now, and I said I was going back to cab driving. And why did I say that? I didn't know the outcome of my meeting with Hogan yet. But I said it because in my mind's eye I saw a long line of funeral homes smiling at me.

"I hope this won't inconvenience you," I told her. "I guess this must be some kind of record for short-term employment."

She just laughed, and told me that the record had been set a long time ago by a kid who had driven for a total of one hour and then quit. He couldn't find an address, so he just parked the van and walked away. I wracked my memory to make sure it wasn't me. The jury is still out.

By the way, just for the record, there were only four deliveries to be made on my last day, so my paycheck for the week came to $192.00. I felt like a first-time novelist staring at his advance from a publisher.

I ceased to be a petal-pusher at high noon. It had been the first job I ever held where people actually broke into smiles when they opened their doors. It made me feel like a hippie. But whichever way the meeting with Hogan went, my trip into the Age of Aquarius was defunct. If the news turned out bad, I would be practicing CM again until I got it right.

I won't insult your intelligence with my coyness anymore. Let's get this over with.

After I arrived at Rocky Cab, I strode past the cage without looking at Rollo. I was officially a civilian right then and didn't come under his somewhat dubious authority. A cage man wields quite a bit of authority in any cab company, but I don't like to talk about that because I don't like to say things about Rollo that make me mad.

"Have a seat, Murph."

I was standing in Hogan's office. I had a hard time interpreting his statement, but I decided that since I was currently enjoying civilian status, the offer did not possess any taint of trouble. After all, Hogan had offered me a seat fourteen years earlier when I had first applied for the job as a driver. Ergo, right at that moment we were equals. With any luck, it wouldn't last.

"We have a few things to talk about here," he said. "First off, I spoke with Detectives Duncan and Argyle, and they filled me in on the business about Mr. Trowbridge still being alive. Also, the insurance company reopened the investigation about your burning cab, and after talking to the firefighters who answered the call that afternoon, they came to the conclusion that the air conditioner motor on your cab was the source of the fire. It overheated and burned out the whole system. This has happened a couple times in the past with other vehicles in the fleet, so you're cleared on that one."

I started to tell Hogan that I hadn't even been using the air conditioner that day, but a little voice inside my head told me to let sleeping dogs lie. I've been hearing that voice ever since I left Wichita. It sounds just like Joanne Woodward's voice. So do the other two voices, but let's move on.

"I had a meeting with the owners yesterday, Murph, and they've agreed to lift your suspension, but with one caveat."

Damn. I knew what was coming next: any new murder charges, and me and Rocky Cab were quits forever.

"It has to do with the blank receipt you gave to Mr. Trowbridge. Like I said before, to me it was a fairly trivial thing, but it was also a technical violation of regulations."

I started to sweat. I can't stand any form of criticism, especially when it's justified.

"I'm sorry to have to say this, Murph, but the violation is going on your permanent record." Hogan pulled open a drawer and withdrew a sheet of paper. He dropped it onto his desk. "I've been ordered to place this written reprimand in your file."

The blood drained from my face. "But … couldn't you just let me off with a verbal reprimand?"

"I brought that up at the meeting with the top brass, Murph. Believe me, I fought hard for you, but they wouldn't go for it."

Fer the luvva Christ. Once again I found myself on the receiving end of The Written Word. How could things have come to such a pass? Why couldn't they have opted for a verbal? The beauty of the verbal reprimand is that it has about as much significance as a Bronco defeat in a pre-season football game. But a written reprimand? In a world filled with

Xerox machines, a guy like me could easily find himself caught up in a web of smirks.

But I kept a short leash on my urge to complain. The top brass had spoken. I knew a few things about brass. I had developed an intimate relationship with brass in the army. You can polish brass, kiss its ass, or hide from it in the latrine—but you can't argue with it, or you might find yourself washing jeeps while your buddies are getting drunk in town. Call me a coward, but I had no desire to become acquainted with the civilian version of general-purpose vehicle maintenance.

"I understand," I said.

"I'm glad you see it that way, Murph."

I was back in. But I told Hogan I wouldn't be driving until Monday, even though I could have gone downstairs and signed out a cab right then. It was Friday, the busiest day of the week. But I had some hard thinking to do. Plus, I'm lazy. It had been fourteen years since I had taken an authentic vacation, and I figured I deserved a three-day spring break, if for no other reason than I always think I deserve special treatment. My ego was somewhat mollified by this attitude—not that I gave a damn.

I drove back to my crow's nest with a fresh coat of bitter victory on my tongue. I figured there was only one way to wash it off: boilermakers. But then, as I turned onto Colfax, I spotted a Starbucks. What the hell. I caved in and bought a mocha. I decided to save the bender until St. Patrick's Day, or my next trip to Sweeney's, whichever came first. I didn't look forward to going to Sweeney's. I figured I would have to bring a written note from Duncan and Argyle before Sweeney would rescind my eighty-six. But that's not what bothered me. It was knowing that I would have to thank Harold for helping save my job that kept me away from the tavern for almost two days. By "almost" I mean Saturday night. It turned out Duncan and Argyle were more than happy to write me a note, especially when I gave them my word that they would never seen me again.

Is that ending happy enough for you?

Well, the story doesn't end there. I returned to work on Monday. My driving schedule got back in synch with my reality. When the rent came due, I worked five days in a row. This meant I spent five mornings sitting outside the Brown Palace reading paperbacks and eating Twinkies. And whenever I happened to drive past a flower delivery truck I hollered "Sucker!" unless I had a fare in the backseat. Then I "thought" it.

The months passed. I checked my answering machine every evening, but it was no-go on the lottery. Things were back to normal. And then one evening the manager of my apartment building knocked on my door. You might think this would have rattled me sufficiently to make me jump out of my skin, but me and the kid who manages the joint have a secret code worked out, since my status as a tenant requires that he visit me every now and then to let the exterminator in. By "secret code" I mean "shave-and-a-haircut."

When I answered the door he was grinning the way he always does. He's in his twenties. His name is Keith. The actual owner of the building is an absentee landlord, thank God. The kid is just a student who goes to a free school, majoring in macrame.

"This has been in your mailbox for a week, Murph," Keith said. "I thought I should let you know. The postman has been asking questions."

I thanked the kid and I meant it. I check my mail only when I'm expecting a refund from the IRS. You do the math.

After I shut the door I headed for the wastebasket. I assumed it was junk mail since the envelope was "funny looking." But then something clicked inside my head: maybe the lottery people used funny-looking envelopes. I finally checked the return address. There wasn't one, but the postmark read "Brazil." I thumbed through my mental Rolodex and tried to recall if I had sent a manuscript to a publisher in Rio. No go.

I'll admit it. I played the envelope game. I sniffed it. I held it up to the light. When I was a kid I used to rip open envelopes immediately, but that's the impetuosity of youth. I once sent away for an instruction pamphlet that promised to teach me how to become a taxidermist in my spare time. I was ten years old. My Maw informed me that I had no spare time.

I finally opened the envelope. I withdrew a single sheet of paper. There was no date and no signature, but there was a message. It was handwritten. It looked like the kind of message that a desperate man might scribble in a lonely room at the end of a deserted hallway at the "Y." I knew who had sent it. I have the unique ability to recognize my own handwriting. It closely resembles that of a man I once knew.

The message went as follows:

"If you are approached by another member of The Heart of Darkness Club who professes the slightest urge to give up smoking, drinking, TV, skipping classes, or admits a desire to hand in homework on time, to go to bed early, develop an exercise program, indulge in career planning, or commit any other act of treason or insanity, you are obligated under these rules to smother his hopes and dreams and ambitions through the utilization of caustic remarks, hooting, catcalls, bitter sarcasm, ridicule, alcohol, drugs, and any other means at hand, hounding him mercilessly until he is brought to his knees and forced to admit that fundamentally life is a joke."

The End

HOME FOR THE
HOLIDAYS

BOOK 4 IN
THE ASPHALT WARRIOR
SERIES

COMING SOON

CHAPTER 1

I was sitting in Rocky Mountain Taxicab #123 outside the Brown Palace Hotel sipping a soda and eating a Twinkie when an elf climbed into my backseat. "Cherry Creek shopping center," he piped.

I put away my snacks, started the engine, dropped my red flag, and pulled out from the curb. This guy had appeared out of nowhere like elves always do, but he was dressed like a department store Santa Claus. I usually hate it when a pedestrian climbs into my taxi. A "pedestrian" is a person who doesn't come out of a hotel, who doesn't phone the cab company ahead of time for a ride, who comes off the sidewalk and hops into your cab and expects you to take him somewhere—which sounds logical but it doesn't ameliorate the sense of gloom that engulfs a cabbie who is praying for a lucrative trip to Denver International Airport, only to see his hopes and dreams shattered by a legal technicality. To put it another way, a hotel cabstand is a designated zone on a city street set aside by the government for the special use of people like myself. Why I think I'm special is a separate issue, but thank God the city thinks so, too.

Fourth Santa this week. Two of them had gone to the Cherry Creek mall, but one of them—and get this—had gone to Southglenn Mall! What the Southglenn Santa was doing in downtown Denver when he was supposed to be dandling tots ten miles away I didn't know and I didn't ask. His nerves weren't up to it, I could tell. We both knew he was going to be late for his gig, but I didn't bring that up. Instead, I made a pretense at bravura taxi driving, which I have been good at for the past seven out of fourteen years of hacking the mean streets of Denver—not good at bravura driving, but pretending to be. This basically involves sudden starts at green lights and jarring stops at red lights. For some reason people think this gets them places faster. It's what I call an "illusion." Being a cab driver is not unlike being a magician, minus the top hat, the cape, the rabbit, and the gorgeous assistant. But you do have an audience.

In my case it's a mobile audience, which normally consists of one person. But an asphalt warrior's job is to put on a socko performance that inspires his audience to tip big.

It turned out the Southglenn Santa ended up ten minutes late for his gig because traffic was heavy that afternoon, but he was so grateful to me for bouncing him off the headliner that he gave me twenty bucks on a fourteen-dollar ride.

Just call me Merlin.

"Which department store?" I asked my Cherry Creek fare.

He knew what I was getting at. Part-time cab drivers and part-time Santas speak the same esperanto.

"Saks," he said. I could smell vodka on his breath. I glanced at my wristwatch. A quarter to one, meaning fifteen minutes until he went back onstage. I figured this without being told. I knew this guy was playing the clock like a quarterback, I could sense it. He stank of desperation. I didn't know what he was doing in downtown Denver and I wasn't about to ask. Maybe he had been at Sweeney's Tavern. Maybe there wasn't any place in Cherry Creek where a man who worked hard entertaining children could sneak a snort at noon. Maybe he didn't want to be spotted by the Cherry Creek authorities. Or maybe—just maybe—he had actual business downtown.

"What are you doing downtown on your lunch hour, if you don't mind my asking?" I said. My curiosity had gotten the best of me again. I have about as much willpower as a baby human.

"Payday," Santa said.

"If you don't mind my asking again, what kind of money can a guy make working as a Santa Claus?"

"Depends on how hard he's willing to work," the guy said.

I looked at him in my rearview mirror. I couldn't tell by his cherry red nose and the twinkle in his eye whether he was shucking or jiving me. "How hard can a Santa Claus possibly work?" I said.

"I could work every day if I wanted to," he said, "but I don't want to."

I liked that answer. I glanced at the mirror. "Let's say I worked every day from Thanksgiving through Christmas, how much money could I sock away?"

"Enough to pay for your stay at Bellevue." I liked that even better.

"Are we talking five figures?" I said.

"Nah. Four figures tops. Maybe six grand. But that's if you work hard and steady. I'll come out of this season with three grand. More than enough to cover Christmas expenses."

"How did you get into this gig?" I said.

We were cruising down 1st Avenue by now. Cherry Creek was looming in the distance. I was trying to milk him for all the info I could gather. I thought I might try pretending to be jolly.

"A friend told me about it," he said. "That's how most of us get into it."

"Is there still time to apply?" I said.

"Nah. You gotta go down to the Santa agency in early November. There's training. You gotta do stuff."

My heart sank a couple inches. I lost interest in becoming jolly. "Not everybody qualifies though," he said.

This caught my interest. I've never been "qualified" to do anything except sit and tap rubber-coated things with my toes. Some people call it "cab driving."

"What are the qualifications?" I said, but I no longer cared. Wave six grand under my nose and my brain goes right out the window. But it always comes home—just like Lassie, only sooner.

"A bushy white beard is the best qualification," he said. "If you have a real beard, you're automatically in."

"What if you don't have a beard?"

"Then you have to answer all kinds of questions."

Interesting concept. If I spent next year not shaving I would be exempt from a test. Why couldn't high school have been like that?

I pulled up in front of the door to Saks Fifth Avenue. Santa leaned forward and handed me a sawbuck and told me to keep the change. I suspected it was the vodka talking but I didn't ask for a translation. When it comes to greenbacks I'm as multilingual as the average non-American.

After Santa walked away I debated whether to hang out at the mall or head back downtown. The Christmas shopping season had arrived and the mall was crawling with customers, which depressed me because it might cause me to decide to stay at the mall and work hard. But then Christmas always depresses me. In this way I think I am normal. Who doesn't get depressed during the holiday season? Who doesn't despair at the thought of making lots of money? It is virtually impossible for a cab driver to earn less than one hundred dollars a day during the Christmas

shopping season. During Christmas, Americans go nuts trying to find somebody to take their money. It's the exact opposite of April 15th.

"Bah humbug," to quote a pro.

I decided to drift back downtown. I would be damned if I was going to get sucked into the mindless whirlpool of crass commercialism. I save that for novel writing.

"Four hundred east First Avenue," the dispatcher said, and my hand grabbed the mike before my brain got back from playing fetch with Timmy. I was driving past four hundred east First right at that moment. See? This is what I hate about Christmas. It's magical.

"One twenty-three!" I barked. I always bark when I know other cabbies are grabbing their mikes. Newbies never stand a chance. It's the old pros I have to outdraw. I don't want to brag, but even Jack Palance couldn't outdraw Shane.

The fare was a young guy who had just undergone a tooth extraction at a dental office on 1st Avenue. I envied him. When I was in college I had a wisdom-tooth pulled, and I was given a prescription for a bottle of narcotic pills which surely have reached the top of the DEA's hit-list by now. I don't remember the name of the pills, nor do I remember how I ended up in Tiajuana. It's probably a long story.

"I need to go to Albertson's and have a prescription filled," the guy said. He looked to be around thirty. He was kind of woozy. The novocaine hadn't punched out for the day yet.

I drove him to the Albertson's at Alameda and Broadway. "What kind of prescription pills are you getting?" I said. It was none of my business, but what's that got to do with my life?

"It's called Tylenol-B," he said.

My heart sank for him. It might as well have been aspirin, but I didn't say anything to the poor sap. I didn't tell him that there had once been a time in this country when prescriptions were written by doctors and not congressmen.

"Powerful drug," I said, hoping to cheer him up. I no longer envied his excruciating pain.

"Really?" he said.

"Tylenol-B?" I said. "I'm scared of that stuff."

His face lit up in my rearview mirror. I crossed my fingers and said a prayer to the patron saint of placebos. Call me a softie but I knew the guy was doomed. The best he could hope for later on was a total absence of pain. Hell, I don't need drugs to reach that plateau. I own a 27-inch color TV.

I waited outside Albertson's while the guy went in to have his prescription filled. From where I sat I could see a store called SightCity!!! That was where I bought my first and last pair of glasses before converting to disposable contact lenses. I still have the glasses. In fact I have two for the price of one. I keep them in a chest of drawers, tucked in the rear next to an overdue library book. After I got the contact lenses I had the urge to throw the glasses away. It was an odd sort of urge, as though I had a craving to clear all the crap out of my life—but if I did that I wouldn't own anything.

The guy came out of Albertson's beaming with anticipation and clutching a little white package. He lived five blocks east of Broadway. I drove him there in silence. I felt guilty. I kept glancing at him in the rearview mirror. He was studying the writing on the package.

Tylenol-B.

Give me a break.

"Have a heavy trip, dude!" I chirped as he got out. He gave me ten bucks on a six-dollar ride. Now I really felt guilty. The word "oregano" kept welling up in my mind. Don't ask me why. I can't cook.

I headed back toward Lincoln Street. I listened to the Rocky radio just to hear the dispatcher hollering street numbers. Everybody in Denver wanted a taxi, but I gritted my teeth and set a course for true north, up Lincoln to 18th and over to the Brown Palace where I intended to wait for a trip to DIA even though nearby bells kept reaching out for me, east 17th, west 15th, Kinko's, the bus station, my God, it was like someone kicked a pop machine and cans were spilling onto the floor. That happened once when I was in the army. All us dogfaces got free sodas that night. The next morning the soda guy showed up and removed the pop machine from the dayroom permanently. End of parable.

There were six cabs in line at the Brown, so I moved on. I followed the road to the Fairmont, but there were seven cabs in line, so I moved on. When I got to the Hilton there were eight cabs parked at the curb, so I moved on. I felt like Country Charlie Rich. My elusive dream was doomed. It looked like I was going to be taking calls off the radio for the rest of the day.

I cursed the cabbies that were hogging the hotels—and I knew who they were, too. They were newbies. They were amateurs. They were *quitters!* They didn't have what it took to compete with the old pros by grabbing mikes and jumping bells, so they opted for the safety and security of the cabstands. I get thoroughly disgusted whenever I run into people just like me.